Also by Amanda Lee

The Quick and the Thread
Stitch Me Deadly
Thread Reckoning

THE LONG STITCH
GOOD NIGHT

AN EMBROIDERY MYSTERY

AMANDA LEE

AN OBSIDIAN MYSTERY

OBSIDIAN
Published by New American Library, a division of
Penguin Group (USA) Inc., 375 Hudson Street,
New York, New York 10014, USA
Penguin Group (Canada), 90 Eglinton Avenue East, Suite 700, Toronto,
Ontario M4P 2Y3, Canada (a division of Pearson Penguin Canada Inc.)
Penguin Books Ltd., 80 Strand, London WC2R 0RL, England
Penguin Ireland, 25 St. Stephen's Green, Dublin 2,
Ireland (a division of Penguin Books Ltd.)
Penguin Group (Australia), 250 Camberwell Road, Camberwell, Victoria 3124,
Australia (a division of Pearson Australia Group Pty. Ltd.)
Penguin Books India Pvt. Ltd., 11 Community Centre, Panchsheel Park,
New Delhi - 110 017, India
Penguin Group (NZ), 67 Apollo Drive, Rosedale, Auckland 0632,
New Zealand (a division of Pearson New Zealand Ltd.)
Penguin Books (South Africa) (Pty.) Ltd., 24 Sturdee Avenue,
Rosebank, Johannesburg 2196, South Africa

Penguin Books Ltd., Registered Offices:
80 Strand, London WC2R 0RL, England

First published by Obsidian, an imprint of New American Library,
a division of Penguin Group (USA) Inc.

First Printing, April 2012
10 9 8 7 6 5 4 3 2 1

ACKNOWLEDGMENTS

As always, I must thank God first and foremost. I thank my beautiful family—Tim, Lianna, and Nicholas—next. They're wonderful and put up with a lot when deadlines sneak up on me. And I'd be horribly remiss if I didn't give a shout-out to Cooper, my own furry "little" muse who almost always helps me write. (He's almost as small as Angus.)

Special thanks go out to Lieutenant Gregg Hastings of the Oregon State Police for his help in understanding the Oregon major crime team units and judicial procedures.

Thank you to my editor, Jessica Wade, who has made me a better writer since we've been working together. (I now hear you in my head as I self-edit!)

Thank you to my agent, Robert Gottlieb, for your guidance, patience, and support.

Great big bear hugs to all of you!

Chapter One

I was ensconced in my favorite red club chair in the Seven-Year Stitch seating area listening to the rain drumming on the roof and the sidewalk. It was Saint Patrick's Day, and I was reading a book on Mountmellick embroidery. I'd ordered several copies of the book on the traditional Irish craft to sell in my embroidery specialty shop this month, and I'd become really interested in it. I was eager to learn the stitches and make something using the technique.

I'd placed the phone on the ottoman in front of me before getting comfortable. My friend Riley Kendall, who was pregnant and had been on bed rest, had a doctor's appointment today, and I was eager to hear how it went.

When the phone rang, I grabbed it quickly. "Seven-Year—"

"Marcy, it's Keith. Riley wanted me to let you know she just checked into the hospital."

"It's time?" I asked, dropping my book onto the floor as I scrambled to my feet.

"Pretty close. We went in for her regular obstetrics appointment, and the doctor thought she should head on over to the birthing center." Riley's husband took a deep breath. "If she doesn't go into labor by tomorrow morning, the doctor plans to induce. I could be holding Laura within a few hours."

Laura was the name he and Riley had chosen for their daughter. She was their first child, and I could hear the anxiety in Keith's voice.

"It'll be great," I said in what I hoped was my most reassuring voice. "Is there anything either you or Riley needs?"

"Your prayers and support," he said.

"You've got it. I'll be leaving for the hospital in—" I checked my watch. It was a little past four, and I closed the shop at five on Fridays. I'd left Angus, my Irish wolfhound, at home playing in the backyard this morning—it hadn't been raining then—but I would still need to swing by, let him inside, and give him some fresh food and water. "—about an hour. Call me if you think of anything you'd like for me to bring."

"Okay. Thanks, Marcy."

After talking with Keith, I called Sadie. She and I were planning on hanging out this evening while Sadie's husband, Blake, attended a Saint Patty's Day/fraternity reunion party thrown by Todd Calloway at the Brew Crew. Blake and Todd had gone to Oregon State University together and had been members of Alpha Sigma Phi. Blake had been chanting their motto all week: *Causa Latet Vis Est Notissima*—which is Latin for *The cause is hidden, the results well-known.* And he'd worn his phoenix-emblazoned sweatshirt at least three times this week. Sadie said every time she washed it, he wore it again. She'd been threatening not to wash it again but said Blake told her, "That's okay. I know how to work a washing machine . . . probably."

Todd might've been as excited about the reunion as Blake was, but I wouldn't know. I hadn't seen him this week. I hadn't seen him much at all since I went to the masquerade ball last month with Ted Nash. Todd asked me after I'd already accepted Ted's invitation. Todd had gone with Keira, a waitress at MacKenzies' Mochas.

Sadie and I had been invited to the party, but

we felt it was really more of a guy thing. So we were going to make dinner and watch a movie at my house.

"MacKenzies' Mochas," answered Blake's cheerful voice.

"Hi, Blake. It's Marcy. Would you care to fix me up a muffin basket and let me speak to Sadie, please?"

"No problem. Anything wrong?"

I usually took muffin baskets to sick people or grieving families. I explained about Keith's call and how I wanted him and Riley to have some food on hand there at the hospital. "I don't think Keith will leave Riley's side for anything . . . at least, not until after the baby is born."

"Can't blame him there. I'll have the basket ready for you in just a few minutes," he said. "And here's my lovely wife."

"From what I could gather from Blake's end of the conversation, you're getting ready to become a fairy godmother, aren't you?" Sadie asked after she'd taken the phone from Blake.

Thanks to my somewhat petite stature and short platinum hair, both Riley's father and uncle had dubbed me Tinkerbell after the blond, diminutive pixie from *Peter Pan*. Her uncle, Captain Moe—who ran a diner in nearby

Depoe Bay—teased that I'd be Laura Kendall's very own fairy godmother.

"It looks like it will be that way pretty soon," I told Sadie. "Riley isn't in labor yet, but given her high blood pressure and the fact that she's been on bed rest for the past month, the doctor has admitted her. If she doesn't go into labor on her own, they plan to induce tomorrow."

"So then you're canceling on me?"

"Only postponing," I said. "I just want to take the muffins by the hospital and check on Riley, and then I'll be on home."

"Cool. I'll go on over to Todd's party with Blake and say hi to a few of their friends. Do you mind swinging by there when you're finished at the hospital? That way, I won't get to your house too early or too late."

I waited for Sadie to reveal her real reason for wanting me to stop by the Brew Crew.

"And you can say hello to Todd—"

There it was.

"—and meet some of his and Blake's fraternity brothers," she finished.

"I don't mind that at all." I paused. "Do you think I should refrain from mentioning Riley's news to Todd?"

Todd and Riley had dated in the past—Sadie went as far as to say Riley had broken Todd's heart, and I sometimes wondered if he was truly over her.

As if reading my mind, Sadie said, "Marce, Riley is yesterday's news to Todd as far as romance is concerned. He'll be thrilled for her." She lowered her voice. "You know it's you he has feelings for now."

"And what about Keira?" I asked.

"She was a last-minute replacement," she said dismissively. "You know that."

Actually, I didn't know that. Todd had dragged his feet on even mentioning the masquerade ball to me, and he *did* mention it only after I accepted Ted's invitation. Had Todd wanted to take me to the ball, he'd have asked earlier. Maybe he'd been waiting for me to have another date so he could ask Keira without hurting my feelings and ticking off Sadie and Blake, who had first introduced Todd and me (and had been hoping for a romance between us) since I moved to Tallulah Falls about five months ago.

I reiterated to Sadie that I'd see her later, and then I ended the call. I sank back into my chair, picked up my book off the floor, and reflected on the past few months.

Since I'd left my accounting position in San Francisco to open an embroidery specialty shop here in Tallulah Falls, Oregon, I'd been drawn to both Todd and Ted. I'd been hurt badly by my former fiancé about a year ago, and I was reluctant to embark upon a serious relationship with either man. I just wanted to casually date, and I thought that was what they wanted too. Todd had been through the breakup with Riley, and Ted was divorced.

But the more I got to know both Ted and Todd, the more I realized that they were both serious-relationship material. And I knew I'd have to risk giving my heart to one of them eventually, but I simply wasn't quite ready to do that.

Of course, that hadn't been much of a problem lately. Todd had been a little remote since the masquerade ball, and I assumed he'd been seeing Keira. Ted had been swamped with his duties as second-in-command of the Tallulah Falls Police Department since Chief Manu Singh was visiting relatives in India. Manu's wife, Rajani—or, more commonly, Reggie—our local librarian, had returned from vacation last week and had told us Manu's uncle had died while they were there. Manu had stayed behind to help the family get his uncle's affairs in order. Reggie was hoping Manu would be back at home within the next week or so.

I tucked my book into my tote bag and then straightened the pillows on the two navy sofas that faced each other in the sit-and-stitch square. The oval-shaped maple coffee table looked good— no smudges—so I decided a quick dusting would suffice. I crossed the black-and-white-tiled floor to the counter and moved Jill, a mannequin who bears a striking resemblance to Marilyn Monroe, so I could get to the cash register. I emptied the till and locked the money in the safe in my office. I usually made my daily deposits the following mornings, since I didn't often get off work before the bank closed in the afternoon.

I stood back and surveyed the rest of the store to make sure I wasn't leaving anything undone. The yarn and embroidery flosses were neatly in their maple bins, the books were carefully aligned, the red and blue braided rug in the seating area didn't need vacuuming, and Jill was wearing a white beret with a four-leaf clover on the side and a KISS ME, I'M IRISH T-shirt. Everything looked super. I was proud of my little shop.

I locked up and headed down the street to MacKenzies' Mochas. Every time I opened the door to MacKenzies' Mochas, I had to wonder if this is what Heaven smelled like: cinnamon, chocolate, vanilla, coffee. I saw that Blake had my muffin basket waiting on the counter.

"Aye, and there's the wee Blake MacKenzie," I said with a horrible attempt at an Irish accent.

Blake wasn't "wee." He was actually about six feet tall, with a broad, sturdy build. With his All-American blond hair and blue eyes, he was a stark contrast to Sadie, his raven-haired, brown-eyed, European-looking wife.

He scoffed. "*You're* calling someone *wee*?"

"It's an Irish thing." I grinned. "Today even Angus O'Ruff is wee."

"A dog as tall as I am and weighing in at about one hundred fifty pounds is wee," he said. "Right." He lapsed into his own terrible accent. "And what've ye been drinkin', lassie?"

"Nothing. I'm just excited about Riley and the fact that it's Friday, and Sadie and I are having a girls' night later," I said. "Just don't you and Todd get into too much trouble tonight at your frat party."

He placed his hand on his chest. "You wound me, me girl." He didn't roll his *r* properly and tried again. "You know, I should be able to do a better Irish accent, given that my last name is MacKenzie."

"You really should."

"Sadie tells me you're stopping by the party," Blake said. "That's good. I know Todd will be happy to see you."

Blake was every bit as transparent as his wife. I spotted Keira—a curvy brunette—walking toward the kitchen with a tray full of empty glasses.

"Will Keira be at the party?" I asked.

"Nope. She's working tonight." Blake smiled, making me wonder if he and Sadie had asked Keira to work just so she wouldn't be at the party.

"Did Sadie make out the schedule?"

He laughed. "You know her too well."

I shook my head and paid Blake for my muffin basket.

"Give my best to Riley and Keith," he said.

"I will. Tell Sadie I'll see her soon."

I took the muffin basket and walked back up the street to where I'd parked my red Jeep. I appreciated Sadie looking out for me—she'd been like a sister to me since we'd roomed together in college—but she didn't have to punish Keira for liking Todd. If they had a connection, then they should be able to date without any interference. I made a mental note to talk with Sadie about that later.

Before I started driving to the hospital, I checked my phone to make sure I didn't have any voice or text messages from Keith asking me to bring something. Nothing. I guessed the muffins would suffice.

When I got to the hospital, I hurried to the maternity ward. The nurse manning the information desk directed me to Riley's room. I noticed the difference in this area of the hospital compared to the other floors. The maternity ward was serene. The walls were painted a neutral beige rather than the icky green of the other floors, and there were beautiful prints lining the hallway.

The heavy wooden door to Riley's room was slightly ajar. I tapped before noticing Keith sitting by the bed holding Riley's hand. They looked like they were part of a painting themselves—one I'd call *Blissful Anticipation*. Both Riley and Keith were dark-haired, tall, and lean—except for Riley's huge baby bump, of course. They were staring into each other's eyes with joy, love, and expectation. I felt a pang. Had I not already made my presence known, I'd have taken the muffin basket and left it at the nurses' station for delivery to the Kendalls later. But Keith was already rising to open the door the rest of the way.

"Come in," he said.

I handed him the muffin basket, and he and Riley both thanked me.

"How are you feeling?" I asked her.

"Nervous," she said. "But otherwise fine."

"I won't keep you," I said. "I only wanted to drop off the muffins. You guys need some time to yourselves." I knew that before long, Riley's mother and uncle and Keith's parents would be arriving at the hospital. Riley's father was serving time in a federal prison for real estate fraud, but I guessed he was as nervous as any of the other grandparents. Maybe more so, since he couldn't be here.

"Thank you," Keith said. "I'll keep you posted."

As I left the hospital, I couldn't help thinking that if my former fiancé David and I had gotten married last year as planned, I might be having our baby now. Of course, I was over David. I'd finally come to realize how very wrong we'd been for each other. But if we'd been as devoted to each other as Riley and Keith were . . . well . . .

I shook off the thought as I drove out of the parking lot. There was no point in imagining what might have been. It was better to think of what could be. I imagined myself in Riley's place—one hand on my stomach where my baby was still resting, one hand being held by . . . Ted? Todd? Someone else?

I realized I could let myself get into a funk

this evening if I wasn't careful. I supposed it was only natural for a woman to feel a maternal pull when she walked into a birthing center. And that time would come for me . . . eventually. For now, I'd have to settle for nurturing Angus. I'd rented the Irish-themed *Ondine* for Sadie and me to watch with him this evening. Before you think I'm completely cuckoo, I don't think Angus will watch a movie—I just want him to know I'm thinking about him and celebrating his nation's holiday. Okay, so maybe I'm a *little* cuckoo.

By the time I arrived at the Brew Crew, the party was in full swing. And loud. Music, laughter, shouting, billiard balls slamming into each other or into the targeted pocket . . . Did I mention it was loud? Several people saluted me with mugs of green beer as I made my way through the crowd. I spotted Sadie standing in front of the bar to my right.

"Sadie!" I shouted.

She turned. "Hi!" She was holding a glass of green . . . liquid.

"What's that?" I asked.

"Believe it or not, it's water."

I wrinkled my nose in distaste.

"It's okay," she assured me. "It's like regular water, only green."

"I'll pass," I said. "Are you ready to go?"

"Yeah. Just let me say good-bye to Blake and Todd." She glanced around the pub until she spotted them sitting at a couple of tables that had been pushed together. "Come with me."

I dutifully followed Sadie as she zigzagged through the people and tables to where Todd, Blake, and their fraternity friends were sitting. Each man had a drink in front of him—most of them had green beers, but one or two had cocktails—and the overall mood appeared to be jolly.

"You *are* coming back to drive Blake home, aren't you?" I asked Sadie.

"Oh, yes," she said. "Guys, Marcy and I are off."

"Aw, come on, don't go," Todd said, his chocolate brown eyes twinkling. "You just got here, Marcy."

"I know," I said. "But I need to go home and check on Angus, and—"

"At least dance with me before you go," he said. He dug in his pocket and retrieved some quarters. "Blake, my man, play us something on the jukebox."

"There's already music playing," I pointed out.

"Sure, but it isn't the kind we can dance to," he said.

He was right about that. The music that was playing—some sort of Irish tune that sounded like a funeral dirge—was not a dance tune. But Blake was already poking quarters into the jukebox, and within seconds, a slow pop song started to play. Todd took me into his arms and spun me into a waltz.

He was wearing jeans and a kelly green button-down shirt. His dark hair brushed against the hand I had at the back of his neck, and I couldn't resist tugging on a wavy curl.

He smiled. "I've missed you, Marcy. Where've you been the past couple of weeks?"

"Across the street," I said. "I have a shop over there. Maybe you've seen it."

"Oh, yeah," he said with a laugh. "I remember it now."

"You should," I teased. "You used to come visit often enough. Now you hurry past on your way to MacKenzies' Mochas."

"Are you being the green-eyed monster on Saint Patrick's Day?"

"Me? Jealous? Nah." I smiled. "Seriously, if you're happy with Keira, I think that's great."

"I'm not happy with Keira. We only went

out once." He stopped dancing. "What about you? Are you happy with Ted?"

"He and I aren't a couple," I said. "Is this really the time and place to discuss all this?"

"Probably not," he said, swaying once again to the music. "But I do want to discuss it . . . later. Come meet some of my frat brothers."

"Okay."

He led me back to the table where Sadie, Blake, and five other men were waiting.

"May I have the next dance?" a tall man with a receding hairline asked.

"Sorry, Graham," Todd said. "I'm afraid the lady has other plans for the evening." He turned to me. "Marcy, this joker is Graham." He gestured around the table, introducing me to the others. There was a rumpled-looking guy who reminded me of a young Peter Falk as Columbo—his name was Charles. Then there was Andy, who appeared to be shy and unassuming behind his black, rectangular glasses. Mark was obviously a bodybuilder, and he sort of reminded me of Denzel Washington. Last was Roberto, a short, olive-skinned man with a mustache and a ready laugh.

"It's nice to meet all of you," I said. "Do most of you live around here, or are you just in town for the reunion?"

Graham, Andy, and Mark were locals. Charles was from Portland, and Roberto lived in Seattle. I told them I hoped to see them again, and then Sadie and I left.

"What did Todd say while he was dancing with you?" Sadie asked as soon as we got out onto the street.

"I could tell you it's none of your business," I said.

"You could, but you're not that cruel. Come on. What did he say?"

I shrugged. "He said he's very happy with Keira, and I wished them well."

"He did not!"

I had to laugh at the way she was standing there gaping at me indignantly. "No, he didn't. But you didn't have to make Keira work so that she couldn't go to Todd's party tonight."

"I didn't," Sadie said. "She *asked* to work because she needed the overtime pay. Her sister's birthday is coming up, and she's been saving to get her something special."

"Oh." I bit my lower lip. "Sorry."

"Apology accepted. But now you have to tell me what he really said."

"He told me he and Keira aren't a couple, and he asked me about Ted. We decided we'd talk about things later." I sighed. "I'm not sure

I want to talk about things later, but I guess it's inevitable."

"Why don't you want to talk about these . . . things?" she asked. "It all sounds pretty vague, if you ask me."

"I don't want to talk about my feelings because I'm still not sure how I feel. I like both men, Sadie. I'm just not sure which one I like best."

She smiled. "You'll figure it out. And since you don't have to make a decision tonight, let's go watch *Almondine*."

"*Ondine*," I corrected. "You're thinking trout."

"I am kinda hungry."

The movie had just ended. Angus was asleep on his back in front of the television. His long gray legs would twitch occasionally, making me wonder what he was chasing. Sadie and I were sitting on my white, overstuffed sofa with an empty popcorn bowl between us. The credits were rolling, and we were debating who looked better scruffy—Colin Farrell, who had starred in this particular movie, or Johnny Depp, who had not. My vote was for Johnny.

"Come on," I said. "Can you beat Johnny

Depp for scruffy, swarthy hotness? Captain Jack Sparrow, Mort Rainey . . . ? Hello?"

Sadie smiled. "While I'll admit—"

The phone rang.

I held up an index finger. "Hold that thought." I answered the phone with a chirpy hello.

"Marcy, I need to speak to Sadie," Blake said.

He sounded odd, so I didn't tease him about drinking too much and needing his ride home. I merely handed Sadie the phone. "It's Blake."

"Are you ready for me to come get you?" she asked.

I watched her smile fade.

"You're *where*? I'll be right there." She turned the phone off and returned it to the table. "He's in jail."

Chapter Two

Sadie and I shared a look of fear and revulsion as we walked through the metal detectors and into the jail. I wondered if the place was always this crowded on Friday nights, or if Saint Patrick's Day and an overabundance of green beer and other liquors was the cause.

Sadie stepped up to the counter where a forty-something female officer with her hair in a tight bun sat staring at a computer screen. "Excuse me," Sadie said. "My husband is here, and I want to see him."

The officer barely glanced up. "What's his name?"

"Blake MacKenzie." Sadie spoke softly, obviously not wanting to announce to everyone within the sound of her voice that her husband had been arrested.

"Excuse me?" the officer asked. "You'll have to speak up."

"Blake MacKenzie," Sadie repeated a little more loudly.

The officer typed what I assumed was Blake's name into the computer. In a moment she instructed, "Wait here. I'll have someone take you back." She pressed an intercom button and called for Deputy Flaherty.

Within just a couple minutes, a red-haired policeman of average height and build arrived. "Mrs. MacKenzie?"

"That's me," Sadie said.

"Right this way," he said.

"Is it okay if my friend comes too?" she asked.

"Sure."

We followed him down a corridor that led to the cells. Prior to going through the door, Deputy Flaherty waved a metal detecting wand over us to further ensure neither of us was carrying a weapon.

"You may talk with your husband for about five minutes," he told Sadie. "There is to be no physical contact, and I'll remain with you while you speak with him." He pressed a button and the door opened automatically.

The nearly deafening din coming from inside the cellblock reminded me of stepping into a dog kennel at an animal shelter. And the similarities didn't end there. As I looked into the eyes of those behind the locked cage doors, I felt compassion for some and fear of others.

And, of course, my heart broke for Blake. Now wearing a standard-issue orange inmate jumpsuit, he sat on a cot in a cell by himself looking hungover and sad. His usually gleaming hair was limp and sweaty. His face brightened a little when he saw Sadie. He stood and hurried over to the bars. "I'm so sorry."

"It's okay," she said. "Let's just get you home."

Blake looked ruefully at Deputy Flaherty and then back at Sadie. "That's not gonna happen, babe. At least, not until Monday."

"What?" Sadie stepped toward the officer until she was nearly nose to nose with him. "I can pay his bail right now. Why can't he leave?"

"Bail hasn't been set," Deputy Flaherty said patiently. "And it won't be set until the judge presides over the arraignment Monday morning."

"Isn't there something you can do?" she demanded. "Someone you can call? I don't know what charges you have him on, but I'm certain this must be a mistake. My husband is a good man."

The officer spread his hands. "I'm sorry. In cases as serious as this, the accused must appear before the judge for the arraignment and bond hearing before there is even a possibility of his being released."

Sadie went back to stand before Blake. "When you called, you said there had been some trouble at the bar. I thought you'd been in a fight or something. What do the police think you've done?"

Blake sighed. "Graham Stott is dead."

She gasped. "Graham? How? What happened?"

"He was shot," Blake said.

Shot? At the bar? What on earth had happened after we'd left? Was Todd okay?

"B-but who? Why?" Sadie's eyes filled with tears.

Blake simply shook his head.

"The police think you had something to do with it?" she asked.

He nodded.

The automatic door swung open, and another uniformed officer—this one short, heavy, and bald—escorted Todd into the cellblock.

"Todd?" I asked, relieved to see that he did appear to be all right. Like Sadie, I was desperately trying to get a handle on what was going on.

He managed a weak smile. I noticed his hands were cuffed.

The officer instructed us to step back while he placed Todd in the cell with Blake. After shutting the door, he had Todd put his hands through the bars so he could remove the cuffs.

Sadie spun around to face Deputy Flaherty. "Will somebody please tell me what's going on here?"

"Mr. MacKenzie and Mr. Calloway have been charged with the murder of Graham Stott," he said.

Sadie, her face drained of color, turned back to Blake. "What . . . what happened?"

"We don't know," Todd said.

"I wasn't talking to you," Sadie said, her eyes boring into her husband's downcast eyes. "What happened?"

"It's like Todd said, we don't know," Blake said.

"How can you *not* know?" Sadie demanded. "You had to have been there, or else you wouldn't be here now."

Deputy Flaherty cleared his throat. "I'm afraid your time is up, Mrs. MacKenzie. You and your friend will have to leave now."

"How can I help?" I asked Todd quickly.

"Go check on the pub. Make sure the manager, Robbie, took the receipts to the bank and put them in the overnight depository. He's probably home by now, but I doubt he's gone to bed yet," Todd said. "I'd also like you to talk to my dad first thing tomorrow morning. I don't want to call him tonight and scare him and Mom to death, but I need his help with this mess. His name is Nolan, and both his and Robbie's—Robert Barlow's—information is in the Rolodex on my desk."

"In your office at the Brew Crew?" I asked as Deputy Flaherty took me by the arm and began nudging me toward the door.

With his other hand, Deputy Flaherty began propelling Sadie out of the cellblock.

"Yes," Todd called.

"I'll take care of it," I said. "Anything else?"

"No." He sighed. "Just—thank you. I appreciate this."

"Blake, I'll be back," Sadie called over her shoulder.

"Not until tomorrow morning," Blake said. "Please. You need your rest."

She scoffed. "Like I'm going to be able to sleep while you're in jail."

"You can sleep with me!" one of the inmates yelled, setting off a round of wolf whistles and catcalls.

"I'll be back in the morning," she shouted to Blake.

Deputy Flaherty escorted Sadie and me back to the lobby.

"I'll go now and see if the police will let me take a look at that Rolodex," I said to Sadie.

"I'll go with you," she said firmly.

"What's the deal with Blake and Todd being charged with murder?" Sadie asked the officer. "That's ridiculous. Graham was their friend."

Deputy Flaherty shrugged. "All I know is that when our men arrived at the Brew Crew to investigate a reported shooting, Graham Stott was dead. The gun used to murder him was registered to Mr. Calloway, but the fingerprints of both Calloway and your husband were on the weapon. And they were alone in the room with the victim."

When Sadie and I arrived at the Brew Crew, the crime scene technicians were still scrutinizing every inch of the pub. There was yellow crime scene tape up as well as a barricade overseen by two officers—one at each end. Sadie tried to barrel past anyway and was threatened with arrest.

"On what charges?" she shouted.

"Trespassing, interfering with the investigation of a crime, tampering with evidence," one of the officers began rattling off.

I spotted Ted and waved both arms to get his attention.

"Something told me I'd be seeing you tonight," he said wryly as he approached Sadie and me. "But I didn't expect you so soon."

Ted looked more unkempt than I'd ever seen him. But, like Johnny Depp, Ted looked good scruffy. His black hair—shot through with a sprinkling of premature gray—was going in all directions, as if he'd been running his hands through it in frustration. There were shadows beneath his cobalt blue eyes, and there was some stubble on his cheeks and chin.

"You're exhausted," I said softly.

He smiled slightly. "I'm okay."

"Of course *you're* okay," Sadie said. "You're not in *jail*. What do you mean having Blake and Todd arrested?"

"They were the only people in the room with the victim after the shots were fired," Ted said in a low, calm voice. "They were still with the deceased when officers arrived on the scene, and the murder weapon was on the floor between them."

"Of course they were with Graham. He was their friend." Sadie anchored her trembling hands to her hips. "Did you even talk with them before having them hauled away, Ted? You know they aren't murderers!"

"That's just it," he said. "They wouldn't say anything—to me or to anyone else." He looked from Sadie to me. "And given the considerable circumstantial evidence, we had to arrest both men." Ted stepped closer to me. "It's not just our department either. Tallulah County's major crime team is involved."

"I don't care if the president of the United States is involved," Sadie said, on the verge of tears. "I want Blake released into my custody tonight. He is *not* staying in that jail!"

Ted looked at me again, an obvious plea for help. I knew from a couple of my more unfortunate incidents here in Tallulah Falls that the major crime team was made up of several detectives and detective supervisors from police agencies throughout the county. They were the best, they were tenacious, and they were sticklers for following the rules.

I patted Sadie's back soothingly. "Everything will be okay."

"Will it?" she asked, whirling to face me. "Will my husband get to come home tonight?"

"It doesn't look that way," I said, glancing at Ted for confirmation. "From what I understood from Deputy Flaherty, Blake and Todd can't be released until they've been before a judge."

"Then I'll find a judge who'll hear their bond testimony tonight," she said adamantly.

"Sadie, think about it," I said. "If you rush things, you might do more harm than good. Get Blake an attorney and go about things the right way."

"She's right," Ted said. "I made sure they were put in a cell together and by themselves. They'll be safe."

Although she still looked mad enough to spit, Sadie nodded slightly.

"May I go inside?" I asked.

Ted shook his head. "Not until Crime Scene finishes up. What do you need?"

I told him I needed the address and phone number of Todd's dad and the night manager. "Nolan Calloway and Robert Barlow. Their information is in the Rolodex on the desk."

"I'll copy it down and bring it back out to you," he said.

"Everything will be all right," I said, trying once again to reassure Sadie. I half expected her to accuse me of siding with Ted, but she was beginning to realize that he'd done only what he had to do.

"Why do you think they refused to talk with anyone?" Sadie asked.

I couldn't imagine why they wouldn't defend themselves. I supposed they weren't talking because they were either hiding something or that one was protecting the other, but I didn't dare say that to Sadie. I found it almost impossible to believe Blake or Todd would intentionally kill someone. Maybe it had been an accident. Maybe neither of them *knew* what had happened.

"I don't know," I said to Sadie. "That's probably the first thing you should try to find out."

She closed her eyes. "Suddenly, I'm so weary, I can barely stand here."

"Why don't we swing by your house and get a few things so you can stay with Angus and me tonight?" I suggested. "You don't need to be alone."

"Thanks. I appreciate that."

Ted returned with the addresses and phone numbers I'd asked for. "Here you go."

"Thank you, Ted." I took the paper from him

and looked at Mr. and Mrs. Calloway's address. "Is 4935 Old Mill Road very far from here?"

"Only about five miles," Ted said.

"Good. Todd asked me to go break the news to his parents in person first thing tomorrow morning."

"Want me to tag along?" he asked quietly.

I glanced out of the corner of my eyes at Sadie. "Probably not a good idea. Sadie is staying overnight with me, and . . . well, I can't imagine Mr. and Mrs. Calloway would be all that pleased to see you either."

"Excellent point," he said. "This might not be the best time to ask, but do you care if I come by the shop with lunch tomorrow? We might be able to put our heads together and figure this thing out."

"That'd be great. Thanks." I squeezed his forearm. "Get some sleep."

"I will . . . eventually."

A few feet away from us, Sadie was alternating between shifting from one foot to another and checking her watch to craning her neck to see if she could see any activity inside the Brew Crew.

"See you tomorrow," I told Ted. I then called to Sadie, "Are you ready?"

"Yes," she said, hurrying over to me. "I need to get someplace where I can think. I have to call someone . . . everyone . . . Blake's parents, an attorney—"

"Sadie, all that can wait until tomorrow morning." I didn't point out the obvious—that *tomorrow morning* was technically only an hour or so away. This day seemed to have dragged on forever. "First things first. Let's get you an overnight bag packed and get you back to my house. There we can work on a game plan and have a good idea of where to start when we get up tomorrow morning."

"Yeah . . . okay."

Sadie and I got into the Jeep, and I drove us to her house. I tried to make small talk—noting that it was a bit warmer now that the rain had stopped and that we might have some sunshine tomorrow—but I could tell it wasn't helping. I was quiet until I pulled into Sadie's driveway, shut off the engine, and turned to look at Sadie.

"Uh-oh," she said.

"What is it?" I asked.

"The light in the bedroom is on."

I shrugged. "Maybe you or Blake forgot to turn it off this morning. I do things like that all the time."

She shook her head. "I always double-check to make sure everything is off."

We got out and walked up the sidewalk to the door. I loved Sadie and Blake's house. If I had to choose one other house on the Oregon Coast to live in other than mine, I'd pick this one. It was a white stucco cottage with a deck that wrapped all the way around the back of the house. The front door had a diamond-paned window that took up half the door. It reminded me of the kind of door you'd see on the classic TV shows *Lassie* and *Green Acres*. It was hard to imagine a farmhouse door on the Oregon coast, but it worked. And the vaulted ceilings were wonderful. It gave the house such an open, airy feel.

Sadie unlocked the door and stepped inside. "I've got a bad feeling about that light being on."

"Seriously?" I asked. "You've *never* gone off and left a light on accidentally? Don't you think you might be feeling nervous because of everything else that's happened tonight?"

"I guess it *is* possible." Still, she didn't sound so sure about that. "Stay here by the door, okay?"

"Wait. What are you doing?"

"I'm going to look around and make sure everything is okay," she said.

"Then I'm coming with you."

She opened the closet and retrieved Blake's softball bat. "Well, if I start swinging, you'd better duck."

I crept along the hall behind her. Her paranoia was rubbing off on me, and now I was getting a bad vibe myself.

She stepped into the kitchen and flipped the light on. The back door was standing open.

Chapter Three

By the time the patrol car pulled into the driveway with its lights flashing and siren blaring, Sadie and I had been cowering in the Jeep with the doors locked for at least fifteen minutes. I was holding a large metal flashlight I'd taken from beneath my seat, and Sadie was still clutching the softball bat.

I recognized Officer Moore—a rookie officer I'd met a few weeks prior—as soon as he stepped out from behind the wheel of the car. I didn't know the young, auburn-haired female officer accompanying him.

Officer Moore approached my side of the Jeep, and I put down my window.

"Ms. Singer, are you okay?" he asked.

"I'm fine, thanks," I said. "Sadie and I are

afraid that whoever broke into the house might still be in there."

"That's unlikely," he said, "but it pays to be cautious. My partner and I will check it out."

His partner had gone to Sadie's side of the Jeep and was talking with her. "We'll do an initial walk-through, Mrs. MacKenzie, to make sure the perpetrator has left the premises. Then we'll take you through the house so you can make a list of missing items."

"Please stay here until we return for you," Officer Moore said. He nodded at his partner, and they strode up the walk to Sadie's front door. Sadie had left the light on in the foyer, but she and I could gauge their progression through the house as other lights came on.

"How're you holding up?" I asked. Sure, it was a stupid question, but the silence was simply too tense. I had to say *something*.

"I just keep hoping I'll wake up," she said.

Her voice cracked, but she didn't give in to tears. She was strong. I admired that, but I also knew Sadie well enough to realize that she was holding it together only until she could be alone and fall apart.

Officer Moore and his partner returned to the driveway. "Mrs. MacKenzie, the house is secure. Please come with us now and inventory any missing belongings."

I got out of the Jeep and followed Sadie up the walk. I wanted to be on hand to at least provide a little moral support if she and Blake had suffered a considerable loss. And I didn't want to be alone in the driveway unprotected while Sadie and the people with the guns, Tasers, and batons were somewhere in the house.

The thought *What else could go wrong?* kept trudging through my mind, but I tried to firmly block it out. I was too afraid I'd get an answer.

Amazingly enough, nothing seemed to be missing from the MacKenzie home. Officers Moore and Dayton—I finally got the name of Officer Moore's partner—believed the robber had fled when he heard us arrive. Officer Moore helped Sadie bar the door and told her it would hold temporarily but that she would need to get a locksmith to see about it first thing tomorrow morning.

"Do you think he'll come back?" Sadie asked.

Officer Dayton said she didn't think so. "We'll patrol the area every half hour or so the rest of the night. But no one would blame you if you chose to stay elsewhere until after you get that door fixed."

"She was planning to stay at my place anyway," I said. "Would you guys mind hanging around for a few more minutes until she gathers her things?"

"Not at all," Officer Moore said.

"I don't know," Sadie said. "Maybe I should stay here, Marce, just to make sure he doesn't come back."

"That's *exactly* why you should come with me," I said. "If Blake was here, it might be different. But . . ." I trailed off, not wanting to underscore the obvious.

"I think Ms. Singer is right," Officer Moore said. "Go with her tonight, and take care of the door tomorrow. Otherwise, you'll worry all night long."

"As if I won't worry anyway," Sadie said with a sigh. "Okay. Give me five minutes."

When Sadie went to the bedroom to pack her duffel, I turned to Officer Moore. "Do you think this break-in could have anything to do with what happened at the Brew Crew tonight?" I whispered.

He glanced toward the hallway before answering. "I don't know. Nobody who has a clue about what went on at the pub is saying a word about it."

By the time we'd arrived back at my house, Sadie seemed to be almost completely deflated. No one could blame her for that, of course, but I thought she'd feel better if she had a plan of action in place.

"Before we go to bed, why don't we work out a game plan for tomorrow?" I suggested as we walked into the kitchen.

Sadie looked at the clock. "It's already one a.m., and we both need to get an early start in the . . . well, later this morning."

"I know. But I might rest a little easier knowing what I have to get done and how I plan on going about it." I took two small, ruled notepads and two pens from the drawer beneath the microwave. Since I also keep Angus's dental care chew bones in there, he sat up expectantly. I handed him one of the bones, and he loped off to the living room with it.

I sat down at the table with my notepad and pen. I placed the other set in front of the chair nearest Sadie. As I started writing, she pulled out the chair and sat down.

On my pad, I wrote:

1) Visit Calloways
2) Visit Riley
3) Talk with Brew Crew manager

I tapped my index finger on number three. "I know I was supposed to call him tonight, but it's too late now. Besides, I feel sure he made the deposit. Don't you?"

She nodded. "Yeah. Robbie's a good guy. If he was supposed to do something, then he probably did it."

"Do you think Todd might open up to me and tell me what went on at the Brew Crew if I stop by there tomorrow morning?" I asked.

"No offense, but I seriously doubt it. He and Blake must be protecting someone." She closed her eyes and massaged her temples. "It just doesn't make any sense to me whatsoever."

"Not to me, either. We need to talk to those other frat guys."

"That's not a bad idea," she said, opening her eyes. "Do you think we should talk with them together or separately?"

"Let's see them individually first so we can compare how their stories line up." I wrote that on my list. "Aren't you writing anything down? Locksmith? Lawyer?"

"I don't think I'll have any trouble remembering those." Still, to humor me, she pulled the notepad and pen closer, took the cap off the pen and wrote, *Get out of parallel universe—find door to wardrobe!*

I woke up at eight o'clock Saturday morning, and the house was quiet. I supposed Sadie might still be sleeping, but it was odd that Angus hadn't bounded into my room to greet me as soon as the alarm went off.

Stifling a yawn, I got out of bed, slipped on my robe, and padded downstairs to the kitchen. There was a note on the table.

> *Hope you slept better than I did. I finally gave up around six o'clock. I'm going on in to the shop. Stop by before you go in to work if you have time. Thanks for being there for me last night. I truly appreciate you. By the way, I fed Angus and let him out into the backyard.*
> *See ya,*
> *Sadie*

I grabbed a diet soda—no time to wait for

coffee to brew—and a granola bar before hurrying back upstairs to get dressed.

As I pulled on my jeans and a sweatshirt, I put my phone on speaker and dialed the hospital to check on Riley. I learned that she'd given birth to a six-pound four-ounce baby girl at just after four o'clock this morning. I thanked the receptionist, ended the call, and put on my sneakers. Riley would be exhausted. I decided to wait until after work to stop by to see her.

I rushed downstairs with my still-unopened granola bar and soda, set them on the counter, and grabbed a treat for Angus. I went outside and gave the dog a quick hug and his treat and told him I'd come back by to get him before opening the shop if I had time. On the way back through the house, I once again snagged my breakfast before hurrying out the front door.

I got in the Jeep and plugged Todd's parents' address into my GPS. While waiting for it to locate a signal, I opened my granola bar and took a bite. I hadn't given much thought to how I might one day meet Mr. and Mrs. Calloway, but I never would have guessed I'd be introducing myself with the news that their son was in jail.

The GPS announced the first step of its directions, and I backed out of the driveway.

I had plenty of time to eat my breakfast en route to the Calloway house. But given the task I was faced with, the trip was over much too quickly. I pulled into the circular driveway of their immaculate Cape Cod–style home and shut off the Jeep's engine. I admired the beautifully landscaped lawn as I tried to get up the nerve to go to the door.

Nolan Calloway stepped outside to get the newspaper. I recognized him because, except for the wire-rimmed glasses and wavy white hair, he looked like Todd. He was wearing jeans and a red pullover. When he spotted the Jeep, he smiled and waved.

I gulped, wiped my hands on the knees of my jeans, and got out of the car. "Good morning, Mr. Calloway. I'm Marcy Singer."

"Marcy! I've heard Todd speak of you often. What brings you by?"

"Actually, Todd sent me," I said. "May we go inside and talk?"

"Of course." His smile faded. "Anything wrong? Is Todd okay?"

"He's fine." And as far as I knew, he was . . . physically, at least.

Mr. Calloway led me into the living room

and called for his wife. "June, Todd's friend Marcy is here!" He turned to me. "May I get you something—coffee, juice?"

"No, thank you."

He sat down on the brown leather sofa and indicated I should also take a seat. I sat on the chair opposite him and noticed the lovely yellow afghan draped over the back of the sofa. I wondered if Todd's mother had made it. Under cheerier circumstances, I'd have asked.

June Calloway came into the living room, sat down beside her husband, and took his hand. She had professionally colored and styled blond hair, and she wore flattering makeup that accentuated her brown eyes. Though casually dressed in jeans and a pale blue sweater, she looked elegant.

"What is it?" Mrs. Calloway asked. "Where's Todd? Why did he send you? Is he all right?"

"There was an incident at the pub last night, and Todd and Blake MacKenzie were arrested," I said.

Both parents appeared noticeably relieved that Todd wasn't in the hospital, but I knew their relief would be short-lived. After all, he was facing a major charge.

"He didn't want to call and upset you last night," I continued. "He asked me to come talk with you today. He said he'd need your help to get out of this mess."

Mr. Calloway frowned and looked down at the floor. Somehow I'd conveyed to him that Todd was in a dire situation. Mrs. Calloway, on the other hand, didn't get it.

"Was it a fight?" she asked. "Does he need bail money?"

I took a deep breath. "Bail hasn't been set. That's to be determined Monday morning after the arraignment."

"What's the charge?" Mr. Calloway asked hoarsely, still staring at the floor.

"Murder," I said quietly.

"What?" Mrs. Calloway cried. "That's impossible! It's a mistake!"

Mr. Calloway raised his head. "June, calm down. Losing our heads won't help our son." He looked at me. "What happened?"

I explained that Graham Stott had been found shot to death and that Todd's gun was on the floor nearby. "Both Todd and Blake were in the room, their fingerprints were on the gun, and neither of them is talking with the police."

Mr. Calloway stood. "Marcy, would you mind driving me to the jail while my wife takes care of a few things here?"

"Not at all."

"Thank you," he said. "June, I need you to call Campbell Whitting and have him get to the jail as soon as possible."

Mrs. Calloway nodded, but she had a vacancy in her tear-filled eyes that made me wonder if she had fully understood what her husband had said to her. Apparently, Mr. Calloway shared my concern.

He stooped down and took her by the shoulders. "June, look at me."

She dutifully lifted her eyes as tears spilled onto her cheeks.

"Everything's gonna be okay," he said gently. "Now, what did I tell you I need for you to do?"

"Call Cam," she whispered.

"That's right. He's the best criminal lawyer in the state." He hugged her. "Todd didn't kill anybody. We know he didn't. And Cam will prove it." He kissed her cheek before he straightened. "Marcy is taking me to see Todd now. As soon as you get everything squared away with Cam, I'd like for you to join me. And have Cam meet me there too, okay?"

She nodded.

I stood and followed Mr. Calloway out to the Jeep. He started firing off questions as soon as we got in and shut the doors.

"How does he look? What's he saying? Had he and Graham been arguing?"

I'd thought he'd only wanted to avoid having two cars at the jail, but I could now see that he'd wanted to speak with me privately.

"He looked fine when I saw him last night," I said. "It didn't appear to me that he'd been in any sort of physical altercation. Plus, they—he and Blake—have been put in a cell together so they won't be bothered by the other inmates. He didn't have the opportunity to say much to me, other than to ask me to come and talk with you and Mrs. Calloway and to make sure Robbie made the deposit."

"Were you at the Brew Crew when Graham was killed?" Mr. Calloway asked.

"No. I was with Blake's wife, Sadie. Blake called her from the jail."

"Well, I wish Todd had called me," he said. "I could've got a quicker jump on this situation. You never answered my question—had he and Graham been arguing?"

"Not that I know of, but Todd didn't say."

He sighed. "Do you have any idea how Graham Stott wound up dead in a room with my son and Blake MacKenzie?"

"No, sir," I said. "But I get the feeling Todd and Blake are protecting someone."

Chapter Four

By the time Angus and I arrived at the store at ten o'clock Saturday morning, I felt as if I'd already put in half a day's work. I'd gone into the jail with Mr. Calloway to say hello to Blake and Todd and to tell Todd I hadn't spoken with Robbie yet but that I'd try to get in touch with him today. Luckily, Robbie had already been to see Todd. He'd assured Todd that everything was fine with the pub, the deposit, and the inventory. And he told Todd he'd open the Brew Crew this evening as usual. Still, Todd was concerned about Robbie's ability to handle a Saturday night crowd on his own, so I promised to check in sometime this evening to see how things were going. Then I'd left Todd to visit with his dad. Had his dad not been there, I'd have begged Todd to tell the police everything he knew. I hoped Mr. Calloway would do that.

Blake had been lying on his cot with his face to the wall, presumably asleep, the entire time I was at the jail. I'd always felt Blake to be so strong, but he looked vulnerable and alone lying there on the cot. I'd be glad when bail was set so he and Todd could go home. But what about the murder investigation itself? What if one or both of them were found guilty? If they were, they could spend the rest of their lives in prison.

That can't happen. They're innocent. I know they are.

After sniffing around the Seven-Year Stitch for a few minutes, Angus found his favorite squeak toy. He picked it up and pranced over to the window to lie in a shaft of sunlight that was penetrating the clouds.

I restocked the yarns and embroidery flosses before retreating to the sit-and-stitch square with the Mountmellick embroidery book. I really needed to decide what I was going to make so I could create a new window display. The ribbon embroidery display from last month was still in the window, and although it had filled my two ribbon embroidery classes with students, I felt it was time for something fresh.

Even though I had the best of intentions, I couldn't concentrate on the intricate stitches as I thumbed through the book, because my thoughts kept turning to Todd, Blake, and Sadie.

I wondered if Todd had confided in either his dad or his attorney what transpired last night. Then I thought about Sadie. Had she found someone to represent Blake? Had she told Blake about the break-in? Had she contacted the locksmith to have him come out and repair the back door? I was debating on whether or not I should call Sadie when Reggie came through the door.

We'd spoken over the phone and communicated through e-mail, but this was the first time I'd seen her in person since she returned from India. "Reggie!" I sprang from my chair to give her a hug. "I'm so happy to see you!"

"It's good to see you, too," Reggie said. "I dropped in to buy some white perle floss, but mainly, I'd like to find out exactly what happened at the Brew Crew last night."

"I'm trying to figure that out myself . . . and so is Ted, a major crime team, and everyone else in Tallulah Falls . . . or, at least, it seems that way."

"I hope Blake and Todd realize what a serious situation they're in." She stepped over to the sit-and-stitch square and took a seat on the navy sofa that faced the window. "The new district attorney just took office after D.A. Burkette retired a few weeks ago. She'll be pursuing this case aggressively in order to try and prove herself."

"Did you hear that Todd and Blake wouldn't talk with police last night?" I asked, resuming my position in the chair next to Reggie. "I can't understand why they wouldn't. They had to realize that not explaining what happened would only hurt their cases."

Reggie shook her head. "I don't know what they were thinking unless they wanted to confer with their attorneys before discussing the situation and whatever part one or both of them might've had in Graham Stott's death."

"You don't think they were actually involved, do you?"

She avoided my eyes. "Do I believe one of them actually *killed* Mr. Stott? No. But things happen unexpectedly and accidentally, Marcy."

Wanting to change the subject, since this particular one was taking a direction I didn't want to explore at the moment, I asked Reggie about Manu and when he was expected home.

"Hopefully, he'll be back within a week to ten days," she said. "Since Manu's father—also

deceased—and his uncle were in business together, his uncle's death has necessitated a dis-
solution and distribution of corporate assets."

"How's Manu's mom taking everything?" I
asked.

"Not well, which is another reason it's taking Manu so long to work everything out. The
uncle was her baby brother," Reggie said. "Manu
would like to bring his mother back to Tallulah
Falls with him, but she'll never agree to it. India is the only home she's ever known. Besides, Manu's younger sisters are there."

"I know he'll be happy to get everything finished up and get back home to you."

She smiled. "Probably not as happy as I'll be
to get him here." She stood. "I've taken up
enough of your time. If you'll get me five
skeins of white perle floss, I'll head back to the
library."

"I'll get you the floss, but I wish you didn't
have to leave so soon." I went to the embroidery thread bins and got the floss.

"I do, too, but I've taken too long of a break
already this morning. Please call me if there's
any way I can help Blake or Todd."

"Thanks," I said. "I will."

After assuring me she'd see me in class

Tuesday evening if not before, and after giving Angus a loving pat on the head, Reggie left.

The rest of the morning passed without incident. I made a few sales—including one of the Mountmellick embroidery books. I'd asked the woman who bought it if she was familiar with the technique. She's said no but that she enjoyed white-on-white embroidery. I made a mental note to mention the Mountmellick embroidery books to Reggie, who was proficient in the Indian white-on-white technique of *chikankari*.

When there was a lull, I called Sadie. My call went directly to voice mail, so I asked her to give me a ring or to come by whenever she got a chance.

Just past noon, Ted arrived with lunch. He brought cheeseburgers and fries from a nearby diner. I guessed he was avoiding MacKenzies' Mochas for obvious reasons.

"Hi," he said, setting the food on the coffee table between the two sofas. He was dressed casually today in jeans and a navy blue sweatshirt. He'd shaved, but he still looked tired.

I got us a couple of sodas from the minifridge in my office and then returned to the sit-and-stitch square and sat across from Ted. "Did you get any rest at all last night?"

He shrugged. "Some. How about you and Sadie?"

"A little. I got more sleep than Sadie. I'm sure you heard about the break-in at Blake and Sadie's house."

"I read Officer Moore's report." He unwrapped his burger. "He said there was nothing missing, so that's good."

"Yeah. It still added insult to injury." I ate a fry. "And I think it really scared Sadie. Do you think the break-in had anything to do with what happened at the pub?"

"It's hard to say. Maybe it was someone who knew Blake and Sadie planned to be out late last night. Then you guys arrived and scared the person off." He looked pensive as he took a bite of his cheeseburger. "I can't imagine anyone involved in last night's shooting would've gone to the MacKenzies' home, though. I mean, what purpose would that have served?"

"I have no idea. It's just strange that the two events would happen on the same night."

"Well, it *was* Saint Patrick's Day, and the beer was flowing like water . . . and not just at the Brew Crew." Ted tossed Angus a fry.

"I can't help feeling that Blake and Todd initially refused to say anything to police because they were protecting someone."

"I agree with you," Ted said. "But I'm afraid that they're protecting each other."

"Reggie was here earlier. She believes the new district attorney will be out to make a name for herself with this case."

"She's spot-on there. Alicia Landers has taken over a traditionally male Tallulah County office, and she's determined to show everyone that she's got what it takes to get the job done." He gave Angus another fry. "She was a tough defense lawyer, and she'll be a ruthless prosecutor."

"You sound as if you're a fan," I commented.

"I am. Law enforcement needs bulldogs who'll go after criminals with a vengeance."

"True . . . but Blake and Todd aren't criminals."

Ted inclined his head slightly. "We don't know that for sure yet, do we?"

"I do. I don't know what happened in that back room of the Brew Crew last night, but I've known Blake for almost ten years. He and Todd aren't murderers."

He took another bite of his cheeseburger. "These burgers are good, aren't they?"

"Yes, they are, but does that abrupt change in subject mean you disagree?" I asked.

"Maybe. I have to be objective and look at all

the facts before jumping to any conclusion. You know that."

"I do know that. Thank you for bringing the burgers."

"You're welcome." He wiped his mouth with his napkin. "I've missed you."

"I've missed you, too. Reggie said Manu should be home in a week or so."

"When he does get back, I'll take you out for a night on the town," he said with a grin.

"I'll look forward to it." Like Ted, I kept my tone light, not sure how serious he was about this "night on the town" plan. I popped a fry into my mouth, and we ate in silence for a few moments.

After we finished eating, I asked Ted if he was familiar with Campbell Whitting.

"I sure am," he said. "He's reputed to be one of the best criminal lawyers in the state."

"I think that's who's going to be representing Todd."

"Good. Of course, he can only help Todd if Todd will help himself. Has Sadie said who she got to represent Blake?"

"No. I haven't talked with her today," I said. "I'm concerned about her."

"She's lucky to have a friend like you." He smiled as he stood. "I'd better get back to the police station. Call me if you need anything."

He tossed our trash in the garbage can on the way out, and I remained sitting on the sofa facing the window. He waved to me as he walked down the street. I raised my hand and felt a twinge of . . . sadness? Regret? Disappointment?

I wondered whether Ted's job was the only thing distancing him from me. Maybe he preferred the hero role and simply didn't like me as well when I wasn't the damsel in distress. I thought back to the night of the masquerade ball and how Ted and I had clowned around at Captain Moe's after our evening at the ball was cut short by an attempt on my life. Ted and I had danced and flirted. . . . We'd had so much fun that I hadn't wanted that night to end . . . well, at least, *that* part of the night.

Then, suddenly, I'm out of danger, and I don't hear from Ted for two weeks. Was it truly the extra responsibilities at work that were keeping him so busy? Or was Ted losing interest in me?

That afternoon, I received a shipment of needlepoint kits I'd been waiting for. They had Mother's Day–, summer-, and patriotic-themed designs. They were adorable, and I expected them to be a hit. As I unpacked the box, I kept falling in love with first one kit and then another. I arranged three kits of each design on hooks on the maple Peg-Board above the embroidery floss bins, and I was taking the rest of the stock to the storeroom when my phone rang. I quickly deposited the box in the storeroom before hurrying back to the sit-and-stitch square where I'd left my phone.

"Hi. Thanks for calling the Seven-Year Stitch."

"Hey, Marce. You sound out of breath. Is everything okay?"

"Riley! Everything's fine with me. How are *you*?"

"I'm great." She chuckled softly. "Laura took her sweet time about getting here. She didn't show up until four ten this morning."

"I heard. That's why I hadn't called you," I said. "I wanted to give you some time to rest. I'll be by after I close up shop today. I can hardly wait to see Laura."

"She's perfect."

"I know she is. Is Keith over the moon?"

Riley laughed again. "Totally. I think some of the nurses and other parents are starting to get tired of his hanging around outside the nursery when Laura isn't in the room with us."

I laughed too. "He's just a proud papa, and he has every right to be. Is there anything you guys need me to bring you when I come to the hospital?"

"No, but there is something you can give me now—information on what happened last night at the Brew Crew. The news reporters aren't saying much of anything."

I explained to Riley that the reporters—if they were like the rest of us—didn't *know* much of anything. I then went on to tell her the circumstances under which Graham Stott was found.

"Neither Blake nor Todd volunteered any information as to what happened," I said. "Or, at least, they hadn't the last I heard."

"Who's their counsel?" she asked.

"I believe Campbell Whitting will be representing Todd."

"That's good," Riley said. "Cam's an excellent attorney. What about Blake?"

"I don't know. I haven't talked with Sadie today. If this Whitting guy is as good as everybody says he is, why can't he represent them both?"

"That would be a lousy idea, Marce. You can't have one guy adequately defend both men."

"Why not?" I asked.

"Because one of them might be guilty." She sighed. "What was Graham doing at that party in the first place? He never got along with the rest of the Alpha Sigs."

"I have no clue," I said. It was disturbing to think that Riley—who'd known all the fraternity brothers and had dated Todd—would think that either Todd or Blake was capable of shooting Graham Stott to death. She knew them both better than I did. Was I simply naïve, or was everyone else cynical?

After talking with Riley, I called Mom. My mom is Beverly Singer, a highly respected Hollywood costume designer. She'd been shooting on location in New York for the past three weeks, but we talked often, and I knew she'd want to know what was going on with Todd, Blake, and Sadie. Mom had known Sadie since she and I had roomed together in college. Besides, I wanted to get Mom's opinion on everything that was happening.

I briefly explained about Todd and Blake being arrested for murder the night before. "Other than Sadie, I seem to be the only person in town who believes the men are innocent, Mom. And I'm not sure she isn't ambivalent about Todd's innocence."

"Well, for one thing, they're both very fortunate to have you in their corner," she said. "I know you'll be stubborn and persistent in doing whatever you can to make sure the truth is revealed. Just be certain you know what that truth is first."

"That's just it," I said. "I don't know the truth because no one will tell me. All I know is that Todd and Blake aren't killers."

"'I don't know how to defend myself—surprised innocence cannot imagine being under suspicion,'" said Mom.

She lost me. "Huh?"

"It's a quote from the French playwright Pierre Corneille," she said. "It implies that one falsely accused cannot fathom a defense because he can't yet understand that his innocence is actually being called into question."

"Um . . . I'm guessing they understood quite well that their innocence was being called into question when those cell doors slammed shut on them last night."

She sighed. "Well, then, maybe their defense is so outrageous that Blake and Todd are trying to gather evidence as to its veracity before they present it to anyone."

"You mean, like the 'one-armed man' defense in *The Fugitive*?"

"Exactly. If that's the case, then their attorneys will need to find whatever or whoever truly killed the man." She paused. "And, love, I know you don't want to hear this, but it's entirely possible that the man was killed in some sort of struggle, or in self-defense, or . . . or something."

"*'Et tu Brute'*? Even *you* think Blake, Todd, or both of them could be guilty of killing Graham Stott?"

"Don't sound so disapproving, Marcella. It's a rare person indeed who deserves our unquestioned trust. Besides, I *did* say it could've been either justifiable or an accident."

"I know. Thanks, Mom."

"Just get the facts, love," she said. "That's all I'm asking. Approach the investigation as a quest for the truth, not as a way to merely prove your friends are innocent."

"Who said I'm investigating?" I asked.

"Oh, please. I've known you all your life," she said. "Give Angus a hug for me."

Chapter Five

Before going home to drop Angus off Saturday afternoon, I put the CLOSED sign in the window, locked the door, and walked down the street to MacKenzies' Mochas. I was concerned about Sadie, since I hadn't heard from her all day, and I wanted to reiterate that I was there for her if she should need me.

I walked in amid utter chaos, and it was only a quarter past five. The coffeehouse doesn't usually get the evening rush until around seven o'clock, but people were standing around shoulder to shoulder. Sadie stood behind the counter. To say she looked harried would be like saying there were a few gallons of water in the Pacific. There were two waitresses helping Sadie behind the counter, and another was busy attending to customers in the dining room.

I slowly muscled my way to the side of the counter to approach Sadie. "Are you okay?"

"I'm fine, Marcy," she snapped. "What do you need?"

"Nothing," I said. "I only came by to see if you're okay. Do you need me to help out for a while? I'd be happy to put on an apron and get to work."

"No, thanks. We've got it, and I don't have time to train you. But if you aren't going to order anything . . ."

She let the sentence hang, but her meaning was painfully clear: Either order or get out. I wasn't ready to leave, though, and I wasn't going to order something I didn't want just so I could talk with my best friend.

"Did the locksmith go out to your house today?" I asked.

"Yes. Everything is fine." She turned and gave the next customer in line a pointed look. "May I take your order, please?"

As the man stepped forward to relay his beverage request to Sadie, he said, "Why do you think your husband shot that guy? Was it over you? You're a beautiful woman."

"I don't think my husband shot anyone," said Sadie coolly. "Your order?"

He ordered a latte and a scone and craned his neck to check Sadie out from behind when she turned to fill his order.

I finally took Sadie's unsubtle hint and left. I walked back up the sidewalk to get Angus, and I marveled over Sadie's behavior. I could understand why she was ticked off at the rest of Tallulah Falls, especially Creepy who'd ordered the latte and the scone. I doubted he was the first of his kind Sadie had encountered today. But I was her best friend. I was being supportive. I even offered to help . . . and *meant* it! I really would have put on an apron and gotten to work. Granted, I didn't know how to work some of the specialty machines, but I could pour coffee, take orders, bus tables, and hand out pastries. How much training would have been involved in *that*?

Had I done or said something last night to offend Sadie? It hadn't seemed that way from the note she'd left on my kitchen table this morning. Had she seen Ted stop by with lunch earlier today and decided I was fraternizing with the enemy? Or was she simply overwhelmed with everything that was happening and was unable to cope?

I unlocked the door to the Seven-Year Stitch and then relocked it after I got inside. Angus began making minijumps at my waist to let me know he was ready to take the short ride home.

I patted his head. "We'll go in just a minute." I went into my office, turned on the light above my desk, and took out my cell phone. I scrolled through my contacts until I found Sadie's mother, Dorothy Van Huss.

I pressed the icon to dial Dorothy's number and was a little surprised by how cheerfully she answered.

"Hi, Mrs. Van Huss," I said. "This is Marcy Singer."

"Marcy! How lovely to hear from you. Is everything all right?"

"Everything is fine with me, Dorothy. I'm just a little concerned about Sadie."

"Why?" Dorothy asked. "Is she sick?"

She didn't know. Sadie's own mother had no idea of her daughter's predicament, much less that of her son-in-law. I gulped.

"Marcy, darling, what is it?" she asked impatiently when I didn't answer.

Granted, Sadie and Dorothy aren't as close as Mom and I, but the woman needed to know what was going on. Still, it wasn't my place to tell her. I wound up saying, "I'm calling because Sadie is stressing out at work, and I really wish I could get her and Blake to take a vacation."

"I'm fussing at them over that very same thing myself all the time," Dorothy said. "Warm weather will be here before you know it, and they should get away now before they feel hemmed in by the summer tourist crowds."

"I agree. I think I'll write down some links to travel sites and see if Sadie will at least take a look at them," I said.

"I'll see if I can give her another nudge myself. Maybe with both of us nagging her, she'll give in." Dorothy laughed.

I joined in her laughter, and I wondered if it sounded as hollow as it felt. I told Dorothy I'd look forward to seeing them the next time she and her husband were in town. That much was true—they were sweet people, and I *would* be glad to see them. It was Sadie finding out I'd called her parents that I was definitely not looking forward to. She'd think I was out of my gourd suggesting to her mother that she and Blake take a vacation, but hopefully she'd understand that I said the first thing I could think of off the top of my head.

After ending the call, I locked up the shop

again and took Angus home. As I poured kibble into his bowl, I wondered for the umpteenth time why Sadie hadn't told her mom and dad about Blake's arrest. After all, they didn't live terribly far from Tallulah Falls, and I expected the case would get statewide news coverage, especially once it went to trial. It would be horrible if Bill and Dorothy heard about the incident during a news broadcast.

I pushed thoughts of Sadie and her unreasonable behavior out of my head and went upstairs to get the blanket I'd embellished for Riley's baby. The blanket was soft white fleece, and I'd embroidered baby blocks with the letters *L* and *K* in the bottom right corner. A spray of pink flowers made a semicircle around the left side of the blocks, and there was a small blue and yellow butterfly to their right. I'd bought the blanket and began working on the embellishments as soon as I'd learned that Riley and Keith were having a baby girl and that they were naming her Laura. I'd been keeping my fingers crossed that the ultrasound hadn't been wrong.

By the time I'd retrieved the blanket and put it into a gift bag with tissue paper, Angus had finished his bowl of food. I let him out into the fenced backyard to play until I got back from running my errands.

*   *   *

Riley looked unbelievably good for a woman who'd given birth just over thirteen hours ago. Her long dark hair was pulled into a sleek side ponytail, she wore diamond stud earrings, and her makeup was flawless.

"You look radiant," I told her.

"Thank you. I *feel* exhausted."

"I brought you—or, actually, Laura—something," I said, handing her the gift bag.

Riley gasped with delight as she took the blanket from the bag. "Marcy, it's gorgeous! I love it!" She placed the blanket on her lap and opened her arms for a hug.

I gingerly embraced her. "Where's everyone else? I'm surprised to find you alone."

"Trust me, the past couple of days I've learned just how rare privacy in a hospital room can be." She smiled. "Don't get me wrong—I truly appreciate all the attention and warm wishes, but I was secretly glad when Uncle Moe left to open the diner, and Mom and Keith's parents went home to get some rest."

"I can imagine." I couldn't really, of course, never having given birth or been in the hospital for any length of time, but it seemed like the right thing to say.

"Laura is in the nursery, and Keith is probably hovering in the hallway outside the viewing window," Riley said.

"Do you mind if I go look in on Laura?" I asked.

"Of course not. I'd mind if you didn't."

"I'll be back by in a few minutes." I left the room and pulled the door closed behind me. I walked down the hall and followed an arrow indicating that the nursery was to the left.

Keith, an older couple, and another man gathered around the window. It was apparent that they were all there to see different babies. Keith noticed me and moved aside so I could get close enough to see. There were five babies in the nursery—two girls and three boys.

"Which one is she?" I asked Keith, scanning the names. He pointed her out just as I spotted the bassinet with the label BABY GIRL KENDALL.

"She's so gorgeous." I glanced around at the other people crowding around. "They all are."

Keith and I continued to gaze at Laura while he quietly told me all about her birth: how brave Riley had been, how he'd cut the umbilical cord, how he could hardly wait for the nurse to clean up Laura so he could place her in Riley's arms. I smiled and nodded, thinking his play-by-play was sort of sweet but a little more than I needed or wanted to know.

A nurse came to the window and pulled the blinds. It was rest time for the babies, I supposed. The elderly couple and the other man went their separate ways, leaving only Keith and me remaining in the hall.

"Laura is precious," I said. "I know how proud you and Riley must be."

"We are. But until I held that baby girl and realized how totally dependent she is on her mom and me, I never fully grasped the concept of responsibility," Keith said. "Tremendous love—love like I'd never known, sure—but also mind-numbing responsibility." He shook his head slightly. "It really made me think about everything I need to do to protect her, you know? Like making sure I have adequate life insurance coverage, for one thing. Take Graham Stott. He was my age, and now he's dead."

"I didn't realize you and Mr. Stott were friends."

He shrugged. "I don't know that I'd call us friends. We were more like business acquaintances. We're—we were—both in health insurance administration, so our paths would cross on occasion. Still, it's hard to believe he's gone.

His death reminds me not to take unnecessary chances though, you know? Especially now that I'm a dad."

"'Unnecessary chances'?" I asked, frowning. Keith made it sound as if Graham had been killed doing some sort of motorcycle stunt. "But he was at a party."

"True, but some parties and some people should be avoided at all costs," he said.

My frown deepened as I tried and failed to follow Keith's logic. "But he was with his buddies . . . his fraternity brothers. Why shouldn't he have gone to the party?"

"Because someone there hated him. . . . Heck, more than one of them hated him. And one hated him enough to kill him."

"And you think he knew that going into the party?" I asked.

"If he didn't, he should have. That bunch has fought for years over petty garbage—in particular, their various relationships with Tawny Milligan."

"Tawny Milligan? Who's she?"

Before he could answer my question, Keith removed his cell phone from his pocket. "Sorry. I need to take this."

His phone had apparently been on vibrate. I knew phones were forbidden in certain areas of the hospital. Either this wasn't one of those areas, or that was some important call.

I waved as Keith turned away and went into a deserted lounge to talk with the person who'd called him. When I went back to speak with Riley, I found her asleep with Laura's new baby blanket still on her lap. I quietly left.

I swung by the Brew Crew to check on Robbie before I went home. Since the crime scene was restricted to the one back room of the pub, police officers had barricaded the entrance to that room only and had allowed the craft brewery to "resume normal operations in order to avoid financial hardship." The barrier was an effective one—it included chains with combination locks to ensure no one could enter the room where Graham Stott had died.

Like MacKenzies' Mochas, the Brew Crew was more crowded than usual for this early on a Saturday. It rapidly became apparent that the "extras" were on hand because they were curious about last night's shooting. In just the few seconds that it took me to get from the door to the bar, I was already tired of hearing the whispered—and some not-so-quiet—speculations: *You think it was over money? Graham's family is loaded, you know.*

*I'd wager that both Blake MacKenzie and Todd Callo-
way have been jealous of Graham Stott ever since they
were in college together. Graham had a lot of enemies—
in fact, I'm surprised he lived as long as he did.*

At last, I was standing in front of Robbie.
"Hi!" I faked a bright smile. "How's it going?"

His chubby, cherubic face sagged with fatigue.
"Frankly, I'll be glad when this night is over."

"Is there anything I can do?"

"Yell 'Fire!'" His lips tipped up slightly. It
was the closest thing to a smile I was going to
get from him this evening, but it was easy to
see why.

I cupped my hands at my mouth as if I were
indeed going to call out, and then I put my
hands down and laughed.

"What can I get you?" he asked.

Remembering Sadie's assertion that I either
order or get out, I opted for a diet soda.

Robbie scooped some ice into a glass and
then poured my drink. "Say, Marcy," he said
softly. "Do you think the judge will let Todd
and Blake out on bail?"

"Of course," I said. "Don't you?"

"I hadn't thought much about it until some
of the folks in here said the judge might hold
the guys in jail until after the trial," said Robbie.

"But that could take months!"

"I know." He blew out a breath. "I don't think I'd be able to run the Brew Crew by my-self for that long."

"Don't you worry. Todd will probably be back here by Monday evening." I sipped my soda. "Most of the people you hear talking are only speculating. They don't know anything more than you or I." Still, I had to admit that I hadn't considered the possibility of the judge denying bail until Robbie brought it up.

He excused himself and went to serve an-other customer. When he came back to check on me a few minutes later, I reiterated my offer to put on an apron and help out.

"Nah. This crew is pretty good, and this is nothing they haven't dealt with before after football games and stuff like that," he said. "We'll be fine, but thanks anyway."

"If you change your mind, just give me a call. I'm pretty sure my number is in Todd's Rolodex." I bit my lower lip. "Speaking of that Rolodex, could I step into his office and look at that for a second?"

"Sure. Is there anyone in particular you want to talk with? Maybe I can help."

"I want to talk with the men who were here last night," I said as quietly as I could speak and still be heard by Robbie. "I want to get to the bottom of what really happened. In fact, maybe you and I could compare notes sometime tomorrow."

"Okay. I'll give you a call." He jerked his head toward the office, indicating I should go ahead and slip in there.

I hurried into the office, closed the door, and quickly found the names and phone numbers for the men who'd attended last night's party. I also found a number for one Tawny Milligan.

When I returned to the bar, I asked Robbie if he'd ever heard of Tawny Milligan.

He actually blushed. "Sort of. Why do you ask?"

"Someone mentioned to me that the fraternity brothers had been fighting over her for years," I said.

"I guess that's true. From what I understand, she hooked up with some or all of them at one time or another." He took his index finger and rubbed at an imperceptible spot on the bar in front of him. "She was"—he cleared his throat—"kind of loose . . . I guess. But I think a couple of the guys really cared about her."

"Were they talking about her last night?"

"Maybe. Her name usually came up whenever any of them got together," he said. "But I was running the bar while Todd was entertaining his friends." He shrugged. "I didn't get in on their conversations."

"Of course not," I said. "Thanks so much for your help. Do call me tomorrow. Maybe I can buy you brunch."

He finally raised his eyes to mine again and smiled. "Thanks, Marcy. I'll call you."

Leaving the Brew Crew, I looked across the street at MacKenzies' Mochas and saw Bill and Dorothy Van Huss going inside.

Sadie's gonna kill me. Sadie's gonna kill me. The internal mantra taunted me as I hurried to the Jeep.

By the time I arrived home, I realized how hungry and tired I was. I ordered a pizza and then sat down in the living room with my list of names and phone numbers. I thought I could probably speak with most of the people on the list in the half hour to forty-five minutes before my pizza arrived, but I had no idea what to say to them.

Hi, I'm Marcy Singer. You met me at the Saint Patrick's Day party. You know, the one where your friend Graham was killed? I'm trying to convince the world that neither Todd nor Blake is responsible for Graham's murder. Can you help me out with that?

I then waffled back and forth as to whether to start with the men—who were at the party—or Tawny Milligan—who, to my knowledge, was not. Maybe it would be easier to talk with her first. I could say I knew she was a friend of Graham's and I was calling to ask whether or not she knew he'd . . . he'd what? Been in an accident? I couldn't come right out and say Graham had died the night before. That would be gauche. Hopefully, she'd have seen a news report about Graham's death and—should she decide to speak with me—could tell me if she thought Blake or Todd had anything to do with Graham's murder.

She could also tell me more about Graham. If he'd been her boyfriend at some point, then she'd likely know more about him than his fraternity brothers and could provide some solid leads Sadie and I could follow.

I punched her number into the phone. I was immediately blasted with the earsplitting beeps that preceded the message: "The number you have dialed has been disconnected or is no longer in service. If you feel you have reached this message in error—"

I ended the call, rechecked the number, and dialed again. Same message. I was still hoping to speak with her before calling the fraternity brothers, so I switched to my phone's Web browser and did a search for the name Tawny Milligan.

I could hardly believe it when a nationwide search of white pages turned up zero matches. Of course, Tawny Milligan did sound like a stage name or something. But where had she gone? She couldn't have simply disappeared.

Chapter Six

Not being able to reach Tawny Milligan, I looked down at the list of names. I'd decided to be subtle in my approach with most of the men. I was afraid that coming right out and asking them about Graham Stott or the events of the previous night would likely scare them and cause them to clam up. They certainly wouldn't want to say anything that would deflect suspicion from Todd and Blake onto themselves. And since they were all still at the Brew Crew when the shooting occurred, they were viable suspects. It was possible that some of them had even retained attorneys who had told them not to speak with anyone about Graham's death.

I perused the list again. I recalled that Andy

was an economics professor at Tallulah County Community College. I ran a small business. That one should be simple. I punched in the number.

"Hello." Andy said only that single word, but it was packed with trepidation and a hint of dread.

"Hi, Andy. This is Marcy Singer. We met at the Brew Crew last night."

"Sure, I remember. You're Sadie's friend." Still cautious.

"Yeah. Anyway, I understand you're an expert on economics," I said.

"I guess you could say that," said Andy.

"Could I make an appointment to see you . . . or could I maybe buy you dinner tomorrow night? I only opened the Seven-Year Stitch a few months ago, and I'd like to pick your brain about what I should be doing to get the most tax breaks this year."

He hesitated before answering. "Don't you have a CPA to advise you on financial matters?"

"Sure, but . . ." I suffered a pang of guilt as I thought of all the years I'd spent in accounting myself and scrambled for a valid-sounding excuse. "Well, as you can imagine, a CPA would charge me a small fortune for this kind of information. I thought maybe you could give me a few pointers to make sure I'm on the right track in exchange for dinner. If you aren't interested, could you recommend someone? One of your students, maybe?" I hoped the addition of asking for a recommendation would assure him I was legitimately seeking information. Which I was . . . just not about tax breaks.

"Uh, no. I mean, yeah. I could meet you for dinner tomorrow night," he said. "Just tell me when and where."

"Great. Thank you," I said. I suggested we meet at a seafood place in Lincoln City, and he agreed to be there at six o'clock.

So far, Sunday was shaping up to be a food-filled day—brunch with Robbie and dinner with Andy. While I was contemplating all the food I'd likely be eating the next day, my pizza arrived. I realized I should've probably made a healthier choice tonight, but it was too late to think about that now. Besides, I was starving.

I took my pizza into the kitchen, grabbed a diet soda from the fridge, and placed two slices of the cheese pizza on a plate. As I bit into the first slice, I saw that the next name on my list was Mark, the personal trainer. Perfect.

When I called Mark, I got his voice mail. I left a message telling him my name and saying that I needed to develop some upper body strength. I said I'd like to make an appointment with him for advice on how to do that.

He called back almost immediately, and I got the impression he thought my request was just a ploy to get to see him again. I tried to explain that since opening the shop and receiving regular shipments of embroidery supplies, I needed to learn to lift the heavy boxes without hurting myself. That was totally true, but he still acted like he was patronizing me when he made me an appointment for Monday after work. If I hadn't wanted to talk with him so badly, I'd have told him to shove his appointment. But I did want whatever information he could give me about Graham, the other guys from the fraternity, and what had happened at the Brew Crew last night.

The next name on my list was Charles. Being a journalist for the *Portland Patriot*, Charles would want the truth too. Surely he'd want to cover the story for his newspaper, especially given his personal interest in the case.

When I called Charles, a child answered the phone. "Hi," I said in my sunniest voice. "May I please speak with your dad?"

"Are you trying to sell us something?" the boy asked suspiciously.

I suppressed a giggle. "No. I'd just like to talk with him for a second about his work."

"You're not trying to *date* him, are you?" he asked.

"No," I said. "I promise, it's strictly business."

"Okay." I heard the phone being set aside. Then, "Dad! Phone!"

In a minute Charles came on the line. "Hello, this is Charlie."

I introduced myself and offered to help him gather information on the case. "I know you'll need a local to do some of the legwork for you, and I'm willing to keep you posted on everything that's going on."

"What's in it for you?" he asked.

The kid obviously came by his skepticism genetically.

"I believe Todd and Blake are innocent. I don't know what happened in that back room of the Brew Crew, but I don't think either of my friends killed Graham Stott. And I intend to prove that."

"That's awfully noble," said Charles. "So what do you need me for?"

"Leverage—so the authorities will listen to me once I learn the truth," I said. "They're far more likely to pay attention to a respected journalist than to an embroidery shop owner. And I'd also like information on Graham Stott."

Charles asked me to meet him Monday evening at a bar in McMinnville, halfway between Tallulah Falls and Portland. I'd have to hurry through my personal training lesson, but I told him I'd be there.

Last on my list was Roberto. When I called him, a woman answered.

"Hi, I'm Marcy Singer. May I please speak with Roberto?"

"May I tell him what you want to talk with him about?" she asked. Judging by her territorial tone, she had to be either Roberto's wife or girlfriend. And it appeared she had some trust issues.

"I run an embroidery shop in Tallulah Falls, and Roberto is a friend of Todd Calloway's. In fact, Todd introduced us last night. I wondered if you guys could use some costuming help." Although I didn't personally do costuming, it was the only even semivalid reason I could come up with to speak with Roberto. The woman didn't answer right away, so—even though I hated myself for doing it—I said, "My mom is Beverly Singer, the Hollywood costume designer." Her sharp intake of breath told me she was familiar with Mom. "While I'm not in the same league as Mom, I'm—"

"Wait," she interrupted excitedly. "Hold on. I'll get Roberto."

In an instant, Roberto had come on the line and said that he and his wife were still in Tallulah Falls—I had called his cell number—and that they'd like to come by the shop and talk with me on Monday. I asked them to come in around lunchtime, since business was usually slower then, and he said he and Carla would be there.

I finished my calls, let Angus inside, and gave him a slice of pizza. I then put the rest of the pizza into the refrigerator. I was getting ready to go upstairs and soak in a nice, hot, scented bath when Ted called.

"How's everything going?" he asked.

"It's going." I took the phone into the living room and stretched out on the sofa.

"It might be going, but it doesn't sound like it's going well."

"Sadie won't talk to me. She's just completely shutting me out." I explained about the coffeehouse incident where she'd made it obvious she wanted me to leave. "I'd help her if she'd let me. When it became apparent she *wouldn't* allow me to help, I called her mom."

He chuckled. "You ratted her out to her mom?"

"It wasn't like that," I protested. "Somebody needed to be there for Sadie. I thought that, since she was pushing me away, she might let her parents in. But—get this—they didn't even know Blake had been arrested."

"This might surprise you," he said, "but not everybody confides in their parents the way you do to your mom."

"But Blake was *arrested*, Ted. For *murder*."

"I know. I was there."

I huffed. "What I mean is, this is serious. Todd . . . I mean, Blake . . . I mean, Todd *and* Blake could go to prison if we can't prove they didn't kill Graham Stott. Sadie had to know her parents would find out eventually. Besides, I didn't *tell* them about Blake. I made some lame comment about Sadie and Blake needing to take a vacation."

"Oh, well, that's different. Sadie's mom would never see through that to determine that something was really wrong."

"Ha, ha. And, you're right—she must've seen through my call or else found out about Blake some other way because I saw her and Sadie's dad going into MacKenzies' Mochas this afternoon."

"Maybe they saw it on the news," Ted said. "The simple fact that nobody knows anything hasn't stopped the media from reporting on it . . . especially since Graham Stott had so much money and influence around here."

"I was only trying to help," I said. "But I probably made matters worse. I owe Sadie an apology. In fact, I should probably hang up now and call her."

"Yeah, I think you probably should. Have a good night and call me if you need anything."

"Thanks. Good night." I ended the call, but I didn't call Sadie. Instead, I cried. Finally, the emotional toll of the past two days had caught up with me. Todd, Blake, or both men could be facing a lifetime in jail, whether they were innocent or not; sometimes innocence couldn't be proven. Sadie wasn't speaking to me. And I had no idea how I could help my friends. I still couldn't fathom why neither Blake nor Todd had spoken up in defense of themselves and their reason for being in that room with a dead man and a gun.

Angus lumbered over and placed his big scruffy head on my knee. As I stroked his fur, I realized Ted had been noncommittal when I mentioned that we needed to prove that Todd and Blake were innocent. Did he truly believe one or both of them were guilty? I had to admit, the guys certainly appeared guilty. But they weren't. I knew in my heart that they weren't murderers.

The doorbell rang. Angus rushed to the door barking, while I followed somewhat slowly and reluctantly. I dried my eyes before looking through the peephole. It was Sadie. I took a deep breath and opened the door.

"I'm here for the stuff I left behind this morning," Sadie said, brushing past me into the living room.

"I don't know what I did to make you so mad at me," I said as I closed the door. "But I realize I didn't help matters by calling your mom and telling her you needed a vacation."

"No, you sure didn't," she said. "She called me after talking with you and grilled me until I broke down and told her about Blake. Now, on top of everything else I have to deal with, I've got houseguests."

"Were you mad earlier today because you saw Ted come by the shop?"

She put her fists on her hips. "I wasn't mad at you, Marcy. Contrary to what you might think, not everyone's actions revolve around you. I hadn't even had time to think about you today. I was doing well to put one foot in front of the other and keep going without breaking down." She sank onto the ottoman that was directly behind her and began sobbing.

My tears were still close enough to the surface that they spilled out all over the place as soon as Sadie's started. Not knowing whether I'd be slapped or embraced but willing to take a chance, I went to Sadie and knelt beside her. She hugged me, and we wept together until Angus came and began licking our faces. Laughing, we pulled away from each other and lavished affection on the lanky dog with the bemused expression.

"I'm sorry," I said at last. "You're right. I *do* tend to think everything is about me."

"No, you were right. I was pushing everyone away today. I didn't want help, and I didn't want to tell Mom and Dad because that made everything more real to me." She wiped her eyes. "I keep waiting for this mess to resolve itself."

"Well, you know me," I said. "*Wait* isn't in my dictionary. I've already scheduled meetings with the four other fraternity brothers who were at the Brew Crew last night." I gave her an abbreviated version of my conversations with the men.

"That's great," Sadie said. "But why did you

tell Charles the truth when you were so cagey with the rest of them? He could have something to hide, too, you know."

"I know, but the only way I felt I could get him to cooperate was to make him feel like he had something to gain as well—the story. Actually, I did that with all of them. I'm buying Andy dinner, paying Mark for a personal training session, and—in a roundabout way—offering Roberto the possibility of networking with my mom or some other Hollywood insiders." I shrugged. "An article was all I had to offer Charles."

"It seems to have worked." She smiled. "Thank you."

"I'll let you know what I find out," I said. "By the way, do you know a woman named Tawny Milligan?"

"The name sounds vaguely familiar. Why?"

"Robbie told me some of the fraternity brothers had spoken about her, and I'd hoped to contact her to see what she could tell me about Graham. The number I got for her from Todd's Rolodex had been disconnected, though."

"We could look her up in the *Beaver*," Sadie said. She laughed when my eyebrows shot up. "It's the name of Oregon State's yearbook. Blake only has the yearbook for the last year he was at school, but if this Tawny chick was friends with some of the fraternity guys, then she had to have gone to the school and should be in the yearbook. Maybe it would at least tell us where she was from, and we would have something to go on."

"I'll mention her to the guys, too," I said. "That is, if I can find a way to work her into the conversation." I smiled. "Maybe I could tell Mark I want biceps like Tawny Milligan's."

"And, with your luck, she'd have the scrawniest little arms imaginable."

I walked toward the Brew Crew. There was a thick fog everywhere, and I could barely see. It was crowded—people were scrambling inside for the free green beer because it was Saint Patrick's Day. I could've sworn I saw a leprechaun. I closed my eyes for a moment, and when I opened them, he was gone. Rats. No gold for me.

I heard gunshots. Oh, no! I had to stop it. . . . I had to keep Graham Stott from being murdered. I had to get to Todd and Blake and tell them . . . something . . . tell them not to get involved . . . tell them to run . . . tell Todd not to invite his fraternity brothers to this party . . . tell him . . . tell them . . .

I stepped inside and saw all these people: Sadie,

Todd, Blake, Ted, Mr. and Mrs. Van Huss, Andy, Mark, Roberto, Charles, Graham . . . Oh, thank goodness! He hadn't been murdered after all. Everything would be all right now. I smiled and said, "Am I glad to see you!"

Suddenly, Mark clanged Graham over the head with a dumbbell. Graham crumpled to the floor as Mark handed the dumbbell to Blake.

No!

The scene shifted, and Graham was once again standing among the crowd. He smiled at me, and I returned his smile, relieved again that he was still living.

"You need to get out of here," I told him, my smile fading. "Somebody wants to kill you."

"I know," he said.

As he uttered those words, Charles took a large number two pencil from his shirt pocket and used it to shoot Graham.

Before I could react, the scene shifted to Roberto, who had a prop gun. The gun actually opened to a flag with BANG *written on it when the trigger was pulled. And yet, this, too, killed Graham.*

Andy bent over Graham's motionless body to strangle him with calculator tape while Blake and Todd laughed.

The fog rolled in, obliterating the scene. I tried to get back to Graham, hoping to revive him, to make everything okay somehow. But when the fog cleared, I was once again standing outside the Brew Crew. This time I was behind the barrier erected by the Tallulah Falls Police Department and the major crime team.

"They didn't do this," I said. "Todd and Blake are innocent."

"Tell that to him," said a uniformed policeman, pointing to Graham Stott, who was standing but still had the calculator tape wrapped around his neck.

Graham looked at me sadly. "He's got a point. How do you explain it? It's almost your quintessential closed-door mystery. Two men are in the room with a dead body and a murder weapon. One of the men has to be the murderer, right?"

"No. It isn't right! The murderer had to get out of that room somehow. Or maybe he—or she— never went in. I just have to figure it out."

And that's when I woke up. I got out of bed and went to the bathroom for a cup of water. While I ran the tap water into my cup, I peered at myself in the mirror. If someone else had access to that back room, how *did* he go undetected by both Todd and Blake? After all, if they'd seen the actual killer, they'd have told the police and wouldn't be in jail now. Right?

Unless they *had* seen the killer and would rather go to jail than say so.

I drank the water and returned to bed. As I settled back under the covers, it dawned on me. There was a bathroom just to the left of that back room. Had the murderer shot Graham Stott, dropped the gun, and then slipped into the bathroom unnoticed? After the shot, both Todd and Blake's attention would have been on Graham. They would have had a delayed reaction to the shooter while their minds processed the fact that Graham had collapsed and was dying, right? Could that delay have given the killer enough time to blend into a crowd or duck into the bathroom? It was worth looking into.

Chapter Seven

I awoke the second time to the phone ringing. My half-open eyes caught sight of the clock, and I saw that it was almost ten on Sunday morning. I could hardly believe I'd slept so late.

"Hello." I tried not to sound groggy but failed big-time.

"Marcy, this is Robbie. Did I wake you up?"

"Actually, yes, but I'm glad you did. Otherwise, I might've slept all day."

"Are you still up for meeting for brunch?" he asked.

"Of course. Can we meet at MacKenzies' Mochas in an hour?"

"I'll be there," he told me.

I replaced the receiver and hopped out of bed. Why hadn't Angus woken me up hours ago?

When I stepped into the hall, I saw why—he was lying there on his back still half asleep. Apparently, I wasn't the only one in the Singer household having trouble dealing with the late hours and emotional turmoil of the past couple of days. He rolled over and yawned.

"You and I need some major R and R," I told him, noticing the sunlight streaming through the guest room window. "After my brunch with Robbie, you and I are heading to the beach."

I showered and put on lavender jeans and a purple T-shirt with a small spray of ribbon embroidery violets at the left shoulder. The outfit was a bold fashion statement for sure, but I thought it was cute. Besides, I didn't want Robbie to overlook me when I went into Mac-Kenzies' Mochas. No fear of that now.

I slid my feet into a pair of platform sandals before quickly drying my hair and lightly applying some makeup. I hurried downstairs and put Angus into the backyard with a bowl of food and some fresh water.

Just as I got into the Jeep, my cell phone rang. I answered it with one hand and put the key into the ignition with the other.

"Marcy, hi, it's Ted. You busy?"

"A little. I'm on my way out."

"I just wanted to apologize for teasing you about ratting Sadie out yesterday," he said. "I was only joking but it was out of line. I know you'd never do anything to hurt Sadie."

"Thanks. I apologized to Sadie last night, and we made up."

"I'm glad." He paused. "You said you're on your way out?"

I realized this was his not-so-subtle way of asking where I was going, but I wasn't sure I wanted to confirm his suspicions that I'd launched my own investigation into Graham Stott's murder.

"That's right," I said. "Why? Were you planning on dropping by or something?"

"No. With the arraignment tomorrow, the D.A. called me in to go over the case."

"So the attorneys were able to get that scheduled for tomorrow?" I asked.

"Yep. Nine a.m.," he said.

"Thanks for telling me. I'd like to be there for Sadie if the arraignment will be over before I need to open the shop."

"They usually take only about five minutes."

"Wow," I said. "I was expecting it to take longer."

"Since Blake and Todd are being arraigned

together, it might take a few minutes longer, but not much," Ted said. "I guess I'll see you there then."

"Yeah, I guess so. Thanks for calling."

We said our good-byes. I started the Jeep and backed out of the driveway. I was afraid I'd be late meeting Robbie, but he pulled into MacKenzies' Mochas' back parking lot just ahead of me. He maneuvered his black pickup truck into an available space, got out, and waited for me at the door to the coffeehouse.

"Are you hungry?" I asked as he held the door open for me.

"Always," he said with a grin. "You?"

"Now that I'm awake enough to consider it, I am."

The waitress who'd gone with Todd to the masquerade ball saw us come in and greeted us. As she showed us to a table, she asked Robbie how Todd was holding up.

"He's doing as well as can be expected," Robbie told Keira.

"I think I'll go by and see him sometime today." Though she was speaking to Robbie, she leveled her brown eyes at me when she mentioned visiting Todd. As if I cared. And even if I did—a little—I wasn't about to let her see that.

"I'm sure he'd appreciate it," Robbie said.

I reminded myself that if Todd and Keira were indeed a couple, then great—I was happy for them. I just had to wonder, though, if I'd put off choosing between Todd and Ted for so long that I'd lost them both. Oh, well. If that was the case, then neither man had been meant for me. Better to find that out now rather than later . . . as I knew all too well from experience.

Keira asked for our drink orders—black coffee for Robbie and my usual low-fat vanilla latte with a hint of cinnamon—and left to get them.

I leaned forward so I could speak quietly to Robbie and still have him hear me. "How in the world did Blake and Todd get themselves into such a predicament? What happened Friday night?"

"Well, you already know everybody at the party was drinking," Robbie told me. "And it seemed like the drunker they got, the rougher they got. Graham especially started arguing with anyone he thought he could pick a fight with."

"What made him do that?" I asked.

He shrugged. "Maybe it's just something he does when he drinks. Different people do different things, you know. Some people cry, some get silly, and some fight."

Keira brought our drinks, took our food orders, and said she'd be back to check on us in a bit. She winked at Robbie. "Let me know if you need anything."

Other than to put my drink in front of me, she'd ignored me. What was up with that? I'd never done anything to her. Besides, I was paying for this meal, so if she wanted a decent tip, she'd better be nicer to me.

After Keira walked away, I resumed my conversation with Robbie. "Did Graham argue with Todd or Blake?"

"He got snippy with both of them. He kept telling Blake that he wanted to buy a MacKenzies' Mochas franchise. Blake said he wasn't interested in opening other shops at this time, but Graham believed everybody would be willing to sell out for a price," Robbie said. "Graham finally got downright belligerent. He said that after all he'd done for Blake that Blake owed him."

"Owed him?" I frowned. "Owed him for what?"

"I don't know. That's all I heard."

"What about Todd?" I asked. "Did he and Graham have words too?"

"Mainly Graham insulted the bar," Robbie told me. "He said the Brew Crew was a lowbrow place and that he wouldn't have taken one step inside the place had he not wanted to reconnect with his fraternity brothers so badly."

"Still, that's just petty stuff. Neither of those arguments seems like a legitimate motive for murder," I said. "What did Graham say to the other men?"

"I don't know. I didn't hear them. I could tell they were all pretty aggravated with him as the party was winding down, but I don't have any of the whys and wherefores," he said. "Like I told you yesterday, I was busy tending bar."

"How about Tawny Milligan? Was she at the party?"

"Not that I know of," said Robbie.

"Did you ever meet her?" I asked.

He shook his head. "She must have been something, though. I think she dated most of them at some time or another."

"Wouldn't that be weird for her as well as for the fraternity guys?" I asked.

"Who knows? I wouldn't want to date a girl all my friends had been out with, but maybe it's a fraternity thing," he said. "If I'm not mistaken, Graham and Sadie dated before she started going out with Blake."

My eyes widened. "Are you serious?"

He nodded. "Yeah. Graham was sort of a love-'em-and-leave-'em kinda guy, from what I understand. He dated a lot of girls back in the day . . . and maybe still does. Or, you know, did."

"I never would've guessed Sadie would've gone out with Graham," I said. "She didn't say a word to me about it. And he doesn't seem her type at all. Of course, the whole time I've known Sadie, she's been with Blake." Why hadn't she told me she'd dated Graham? Maybe Blake hadn't known about her and Graham. Realizing I was staring into space like an idiot, I smiled at Robbie. "Oh, well. I guess we all do crazy stuff while we're in college."

"I didn't go to college," Robbie said. "And after watching those guys Friday night, I'm glad I didn't. My friends are my friends— not a bunch of backstabbers."

I rested my chin on my fist. "Robbie, who do you think killed Graham?"

He looked into my eyes before directing his gaze down at the table. "I think it was Blake. And I think Todd isn't saying anything because he's trying to figure out a way to help him."

Unfortunately, neither Robbie nor I had heard or seen Sadie approach our table.

"If anyone's covering for anyone," she said hotly, "it's Blake covering for Todd." She untied her apron. "In fact, I'm going to that jail right now, and I'm demanding that Blake tell the truth and defend himself!" She stormed out of the coffeehouse.

Brunch kinda went downhill after that.

I'd exchanged my sandals for canvas sneakers before Angus and I headed to the beach. We'd been there a half hour. He'd tired of playing fetch with his ball and was now romping to and from the water's edge as I stitched a small cross-stitch cupcake for a birthday card. I didn't know anyone who was having a birthday today. But I had a book of designs that took only a couple of hours to stitch, and I made them when hauling around a larger project wasn't feasible so that I always had finished cards ready whenever an event came up.

I kept thinking about brunch. Did Robbie really believe Blake had killed Graham? If so, what would make him think that? I also kept thinking about what Robbie said about Sadie and Graham. I wanted to ask Sadie if it was true that she'd dated Graham before she started going out with Blake. If I spoke with her about that, though, I had better tread carefully. I didn't want her to think for an instant that *I* thought Blake had murdered Graham.

Even if Sadie *had* dated Graham, that wouldn't provide a motive for Blake to murder Graham after all this time. He and Sadie had been married for five years, for goodness' sake. And they'd dated for two years before they married.

On the other hand, I could easily see why both Robbie and Sadie would believe Todd and Blake would cover for each other, even in a circumstance like this. They'd been best friends forever and seemed more like brothers than buddies. Plus, it wouldn't be the first time since I've known them that one of them had lied to protect the other.

But Sadie and I had been friends for years, too. Would I cover for her if I thought she'd committed a murder? I mulled that over for a moment and came to the conclusion that I would if I believed she had a good enough reason for doing what she'd done. I'd at least keep quiet until I could get her side of the story. And that's exactly what Todd and Blake were doing.

My phone rang. I removed it from my pocket and checked the screen.

"Hi, Mom," I answered.

"Hello, love. Am I hearing waves?"

"You sure are."

"Actual waves or one of those white noise machine thingies?" she asked.

"Real, live, honest-to-Pete waves," I said with a laugh.

"Good. Then you're relaxing and not out playing detective. So, have you made any progress?"

I told her about setting up meetings with the fraternity brothers and about my brunch with Robbie.

"It sounds as if you have a pretty solid game plan. This Tawny Milligan seems to be a real character," Mom said. "It's too bad you've not been able to find her yet. Or maybe it isn't. I'm not sure you'd want to hear what she might have to tell you."

"What do you mean?" I asked.

"Well, the odds are good that she dated either Blake, Todd, or both. Since you and Todd have dated, I doubt you'd be keen on hearing about their love life. And I *know* Sadie wouldn't want to know about Tawny's past with Blake."

"You're right," I said. "And if she and Blake dated, I don't think Sadie knows about it. She told me the name sounded vaguely familiar, but that's all she seemed to know about Tawny Milligan. If I'm able to find Tawny, I'll tell her I'm not interested in which guys she dated— only what she can tell me about their relationships with Graham Stott."

"You think Tawny Milligan could be a stage name?" Mom cleared her throat. "It sounds a little sleazy, if you ask me."

"I suppose anything is possible." I sighed. "Are you thinking she's an exotic dancer or something?"

"You said it yourself—anything's possible. But if you do track this woman down, won't you be the teeniest bit curious as to whether or not she and Todd dated?" Mom asked.

"Yes, but I'm afraid the Todd ship—and the Ted ship, too, for that matter—might've already left the dock without me," I said.

"What would make you think that?"

I explained how Todd had told me on Friday evening that he and Keira weren't a couple. "But she certainly didn't act that way at Mac-Kenzies' Mochas today. She made it clear that she was going to visit Todd in jail and that she was very much into him."

"Just because she feels that way about him doesn't mean the feeling is mutual," said Mom. "What about Ted?"

"He's had a lot of extra work since Manu has been in India, and he seems distant. It makes me think there's something more going on other than his not having enough time to take more of an interest in me." I threw out my theory that Ted liked me only when I was a damsel in distress.

"Lots of men—I'd say *most* men—enjoy being a hero, love, especially to women they care about. Give him some time and see how he acts after Manu returns. Who knows? Maybe he's under the impression that you're only interested in him when you need a hero."

"Hmm, I hadn't thought of that," I said.

"In the meantime, allow him to do something heroic whenever he's around . . . even if it's just opening a pickle jar for you. And be patient. It'll all work out. All of it."

"I hope you're right, Mom."

"I always am." I could hear the smile in her voice.

I desperately wished I could be as confident as she was.

After Angus and I got home from playing on the beach, he curled up in a corner of the living room to take a nap. Napping actually sounded like a winning idea to me, but I was afraid if I did I'd have insomnia that night. Plus, I didn't want to oversleep and be late getting ready for my dinner date with Andy.

I got my tote bag containing my work in progress and began stitching on my Mountmellick embroidery piece. I'd secured a piece of white denim cloth inside a medium-sized round embroidery hoop, and I was using a pattern featuring shamrocks and daisies. Both required mostly satin stitches and French knots, and I was happy I could try something new while still staying within my comfort zone.

I worked for nearly two hours. It was so peaceful and quiet. The only sound in the house was that of Angus snoring softly. For a little while, it was easy to pretend that all was right with the world and that I had plenty more to be satisfied about than a few shamrocks and three-fourths of a daisy.

I stretched, massaged my hands, and stood up. Angus grunted and rolled over. I rubbed his belly before going upstairs to get dressed.

I didn't want Andy to think I was interested in anything other than information from him— although he might assume that if he found out I had been an accountant before I moved to

Tallulah Falls to open the Seven-Year Stitch—but I didn't want to look dowdy either. I decided to think like Mom. How would she dress me for this scene if I were in a movie? Audrey Hepburn. She'd definitely go with more of an Audrey look than a Marilyn look.

I chose a black dress with a ballerina neckline and an A-line skirt. I didn't have any flats other than casual shoes, but I chose the lowest-heeled black pumps in my closet—a mere three inches. I was the personification of demure.

And yet, Andy still greeted me at the restaurant with a single white rose and a kiss on the hand. And, no, I didn't tell him, "A kiss on the hand may be quite continental, but diamonds are a girl's best friend." I was being Audrey, not Marilyn, remember?

Chapter Eight

"I have to tell you," Andy said after we sat down, "I'm flattered you went to such lengths to go out with me. I asked Keira from MacKenzies' Mochas about you earlier today, and she told me you were an accountant before you came to Tallulah Falls to open your shop."

Busted! Darn that Keira! Now what? I supposed I'd have to shoot straight with him.

I gently placed the rose to the right of my water glass. "I did want to meet with you very much, Andy. But it was because I want your insight on what happened at the Brew Crew on Friday night. I'm trying to help Blake and Todd."

"Oh." He adjusted his glasses. "Oh, of course." He gave a nervous chuckle. "As if a girl like you would ever be interested in a guy like me, right?"

"That's not it at all," I said quickly, wondering if he was really that insecure or if it was an act. "Why *wouldn't* a girl like me be interested in you? You're charming, attractive, intelligent. . . . But right now two of my friends are in jail, and I think they're innocent."

The waiter arrived to take our orders, and we had to ask him to give us a moment because neither of us had even picked up the menu yet. The waiter rattled off the catch of the day and other specials. I decided on lobster ravioli, and Andy chose that dish as well.

"So, under different circumstances, you could see this as a real date?" Andy asked as soon as the waiter left.

"Sure."

He smiled. "Great. That makes me feel a lot less foolish."

"If anyone should feel foolish, it's me," I said. "I'm the one who lied to get you to meet with me. I was afraid you wouldn't open up to me if I told you the real reason I wanted to talk with you."

"Why not?"

I shrugged. "I figured most people wouldn't want to get involved in a murder investigation.

Maybe they'd be afraid of saying something that would get someone in trouble or that would implicate the wrong person . . . that sort of thing."

"But you aren't a police officer," Andy said. "It's not like anything I say can and will be used against me in a court of law." He gave another chuckle. "Right?"

"That's true." I smiled. "But before we start talking about Friday night, tell me about your college days. How did you come to join the Alpha Sigma Phi fraternity?" Maybe a little background about the school would help me get a feel for the fraternity and would also help both Andy and me relax before we dove into the subject of murder.

"I'd come from a small town in Washington, and I didn't know anyone when I first got to OSU," said Andy. "That was hard on me. I wanted to fit in more than anything . . . you know?"

"I can certainly identify with that," I said.

"I thought joining the Alpha Sigs would give me"—he sighed—"I don't know . . . a home base, I guess . . . a place where I knew some guys, they knew me, and I belonged . . . whether we were truly friends or not."

"And did the fraternity help you fit in?" I asked.

"Yeah. At first, I was more like the frat dork than anything. I helped the other guys with their homework, tutored them, stuff like that." He took a long drink from his water glass, and I wondered if he'd truly been happy in his role at the fraternity or if he was merely trying to convince himself of that now.

"Based on the group I met at the Brew Crew, no two of you were that much alike. I'm thinking the fraternity must've been made up of guys with a diverse set of backgrounds, interests, and career goals," I said.

"It was," he said. "And it wasn't like everyone was a jock or a social climber either. I mean, yeah, a lot of them were—and that's why they were in the fraternity—but there were a bunch of good, solid people in the Alpha Sigs, too."

"Like Blake and Todd and the other men at Friday night's party?" I asked.

"Blake and Todd are stand-up guys. A couple of the others I'm not so sure about," he said. "Including Graham."

"Why didn't you care for Graham?" When Andy was silent, I pressed on. "Is it because you had both dated Tawny Milligan?"

Andy's entire face turned red. I wasn't sure if it was from embarrassment, anger, or both.

He lowered his eyes. "Who told you about Tawny?"

"Keith Kendall and Robbie, the bartender from the Brew Crew, mentioned her. What was she like?" I asked.

He still didn't raise his eyes. "She was just a girl who cleaned the frat house for us every other day."

"Was she—"

"I don't want to talk about Tawny. Could we change the subject, please?" His voice was polite, but there was a definite edge to it.

"By all means," I said. "I'm sorry. I didn't intend to upset you. Let's talk about Friday night. What happened leading up to Graham's death?"

"Graham kept drinking and drinking." At last, Andy raised his eyes to mine again. "He never did know when to quit anything. Anyway, the more he drank, the more of a jerk he became to the rest of us. He made fun of everybody . . . He tried to make stupid business deals. . . ." He shook his head. "We all got fed up with him. Todd told him it was time for him to leave. I heard Todd mention calling Graham a cab, and then I saw Todd start toward his office."

"How did Todd wind up in the back room?"

I asked. "Did he go in there after he made the call?"

"No, Graham headed him off and sort of muscled him into the back room," said Andy. "They were still arguing."

"And then what happened?"

"I don't know. I went in the other direction, saw some people I used to work with," he said. "And, yes, they can confirm that."

"I'm sorry," I said, surprised he'd become so defensive. "I didn't mean to come across as Sherlock Holmes or Nancy Drew."

"It's okay," Andy said. "I didn't mean to be so touchy." He was quiet for a moment, and then he brightened. "Hey, have you ever considered the work opportunity tax credit?"

"I'm afraid my only employee is a volunteer—and a mannequin—so she doesn't help me qualify for that tax break," I said with a grin. I got the message. Andy had said all he was willing to about Friday night and the people from his college days.

When I got home, I put the rose in a bud vase on the kitchen counter and then let Angus out into the backyard for a few minutes. I went into the living room, slipped off my shoes, and curled up on the sofa. I called Sadie to ask how things had gone with Blake at the jail and to tell her about dinner with Andy.

Sadie's mom answered the phone. She reiterated how very glad she and Bill were that I'd called. Otherwise, who knew when Sadie would have gotten around to telling them about Blake's wretched predicament? Her minitirade made me feel badly all over again about calling them.

At last, Mrs. Van Huss put Sadie on the phone. Instead of apologizing to Sadie again, which was my initial inclination, I immediately asked about Blake.

"He still refuses to tell me anything," she said quietly. I guessed she didn't want her mother to overhear. "It's infuriating, but he says he can't talk freely there and will tell me everything as soon as he can." She sighed. "So how was your dinner with Andy?"

"Thanks to your oh-so-thoughtful waitress Keira, Andy knew when I arrived that I had a background in accounting. Naturally, he thought I'd concocted this clever ruse in order to ask him out," I said.

Sadie's laughter was a welcome sound, especially given her current stress level, so I tried to keep it going.

"When I arrived at the restaurant, he gallantly presented me with a single white rose and a kiss on the hand," I continued.

"No way," she said, still giggling.

"I have the rose right here to prove it. Come see for yourself if you don't believe me."

"But why not a red rose? Aren't white roses supposed to symbolize friendship or purity or something?" she asked.

"It was our first date, Sadie. He didn't want to rush into anything."

When she stopped laughing over that comment, she asked, "So, how did you play it?"

"I told him the truth—that I wanted to talk with him about the shooting at the Brew Crew."

"What did he say to that?"

"He told me Graham got drunk and started being a jerk to everyone else," I said. "Todd started into his office to call a cab for Graham, but the two of them wound up in the back room. Andy says he didn't see what happened after that."

"You sound skeptical."

"I guess I am, a little. Plus, get this," I said. "When I mentioned Tawny Milligan, he refused to talk about her at all. He completely shut down and asked me to change the subject."

"That's weird," Sadie said.

"Tell me about it. Did you find her photo in the *Beaver*? I really want to get a look at this woman."

"No, I didn't find her photo because I didn't find the *Beaver*. That's another weird thing," she said. "You know how I thought nothing had been stolen from the house during last night's break-in? Well, Blake's copy of the yearbook and all his OSU alumni newsletters are gone. He kept them all together in a file drawer, and when I went to get the yearbook, I saw that everything was gone."

"Do you think maybe Blake moved them or threw them away?" I asked.

"I believe it would be a huge coincidence if he did," she said. "Don't you?"

"Well, yeah. Who else knew where Blake kept those things?"

"Everyone and no one, I suppose." She expelled a breath of frustration. "I mean, it wasn't a secret. The file cabinet was labeled."

"But who—other than one of the fraternity brothers—would want that stuff?" I asked. "It had to be one of them who broke in. And whoever it was *has* to be trying to hide something from their OSU days."

"Like what, Marce? That's quite a stretch. I

mean, we can go online and order another copy of the yearbook. And all the back issues of the newsletter are archived on the Web site," said Sadie. "Nobody is hiding anything by stealing those."

"I guess that's true. But still, I think we need to order that year's issue of the *Beaver* and also find out if there's anything about any of those frat guys mentioned in the newsletters," I said.

"Before we can do that, we'll need to get Blake's username and password." A note of unease crept into her voice.

"You won't need those until tomorrow. It's too late to start work on it tonight. Maybe you can get to it after the bail hearing. Or Blake can log on to the site himself." I was trying to sound reassuring, but I think I was missing the mark.

"I hope you're right."

I infused my voice with as much cheerfulness as I could muster. "Of course I'm right. Why wouldn't I be?"

"The judge might deny bail," she said.

"That won't happen. Blake and Todd are upstanding citizens. They'll be granted bail." I said a silent prayer that I wasn't lying to my best friend.

*   *   *

I got to the courthouse at about eight forty-five Monday morning. I'd left Angus at home in the backyard. Even though it was raining, he could lounge on the porch swing. He liked to snooze there on rainy days. I hoped to have time to go back and get him after the arraignment, but that would depend on the court's schedule and if the arraignment proceeded as quickly as Ted had said it would.

I'd worn dark jeans, taupe pumps, and a lacy beige long-sleeved top. I hadn't wanted to appear overly casual for court, but I hadn't wanted to get dressed up either. This wasn't *my* arraignment. Besides, I had to wear this outfit all day—and it was going to be a long one. Even though I didn't have a class this evening, I was meeting with Mark, the personal trainer, and with Charles, the journalist, after work.

I walked into the courtroom and spotted Sadie. She was sitting near the front with her mom and dad. Sadie shares her mom's dark coloring and her dad's height. Under other circumstances, I might've reminded her she got the best of both worlds as far as her parents' genes went.

Even from behind, I could assess the trio's roles. Sadie's back was straight in her navy suit, and her head was held high. She was being strong for her husband, for herself, and—thanks to me—for her parents. Her mother was bent forward, weeping into a tissue. She was wearing black, as if she were at a funeral. Sadie's dad had his arm around his wife and was patting her shoulder and whispering to her.

I slid onto the bench beside Sadie. "I'm so sorry."

We'd known each other long enough that she knew I was talking about her parents rather than the arraignment, and she rolled her eyes. "It's okay. It's a distraction if nothing else."

I was thinking it was a *sideshow*, but I didn't say so. Instead, I looked toward the tables in front of the judge's bench. "Where are Blake and Todd?"

"They're in the prisoner holding area," Sadie said. "They aren't allowed into the courtroom until their case is called. Those are their lawyers."

"Which one's which?" I whispered.

"The heavyset guy with the bushy gray hair and beard is Todd's lawyer, Campbell Whitting. The skinny one with the bad comb-over is ours—Harry McQuiston."

"Who's she?" I asked, nodding toward the other table at the woman in the red skirt and white silk blouse. She wore red and white spectator pumps, and her dark brown corkscrew curls were held captive by a large black barrette.

"That's District Attorney Landers," Sadie said. "I've heard her called a pit bull in pumps."

"She looks nice enough." I was trying to be helpful and pretend that the rumors I'd heard about Alicia Landers were overblown.

"Looks can be deceiving."

Mrs. Van Huss leaned across in front of Sadie to tell me hello. "So nice of you to come and support the family in our hour of need," she said, reaching over to squeeze my hand.

Rather at a loss for words, I mumbled, "Good to see you." Not wanting to get into a conversation with Mrs. Van Huss, I looked around to see if Ted was in the courtroom. If he was, I couldn't see him.

District Attorney Landers walked over to the defense counsel table, and she and the two defense lawyers exchanged some quiet conversation. It appeared to me that Mr. Whitting took the lead over Mr. McQuiston and that McQuiston was happy to have him do it.

I wondered if McQuiston viewed Whitting as his superior. After all, Whitting did have a stellar reputation. I hadn't heard anything good or bad about Mr. McQuiston. Still, it concerned me that Sadie and Blake hadn't retained a more aggressive attorney.

"How did you find Mr. McQuiston?" I asked Sadie.

Mrs. Van Huss overheard and answered my question. "He's been a friend of our family for years. He did our wills."

"Oh," I said. I wanted to ask if Mr. McQuiston was well versed in criminal law, but that would be rude. Sadie's parents wouldn't knowingly have had her hire someone incompetent to represent Blake. Still, this was his *life* hanging in the balance.

District Attorney Landers returned to her table and busied herself straightening papers. Whitting checked his phone, and McQuiston looked nervous.

A uniformed bailiff walked into the courtroom and told us to stand as the judge entered.

"The Honorable Warren Street presiding," the bailiff announced. As soon as the judge took his seat, the bailiff told us we could be seated.

"The People versus Todd Calloway and Blake

McKenzie," the bailiff called. "Docket number two four seven three nine."

He went to a door at the right of the courtroom and brought out Blake and Todd, whose hands were cuffed in front of them. The bailiff led them to stand before the judge's bench. The guys still wore those awful orange jumpsuits, and they looked pale and tired. I took Sadie's hand as Mrs. Van Huss sobbed into her husband's shoulder.

The judge, a man who was in his mid- to late fifties, with sandy hair and tortoiseshell glasses, asked, "Do the defense attorneys waive the reading of the charges in this matter?"

"We do, Your Honor," Campbell Whitting said.

I had looked up arraignments online last night, and I knew it was common for the reading of the charges to be waived. I suppose it was simply seen as a waste of time, since everyone already knew why they were in court.

The judge thumbed through a file before asking Alicia Landers to provide the specifics of the case.

District Attorney Landers stood and stepped in front of her table. "Your Honor, on Friday evening, March 17, the two defendants were found standing over the body of Graham Stott, who was deceased upon deputies' arrival. Police found a gun at the scene, and it is currently being tested to determine whether or not it was used to shoot the victim, who had suffered fatal gunshot wounds. Upon refusing to answer investigators' questions about how the shooting occurred, Mr. Calloway and Mr. MacKenzie were arrested and charged with first-degree murder."

"Gentlemen, how do you plead?" Judge Street asked.

"My client, Todd Calloway, pleads not guilty," Mr. Whitting said.

"My client, Blake MacKenzie, also pleads not guilty," Mr. McQuiston said.

"Very well. D.A. Landers, what do you propose in the way of bail?" Judge Street asked.

"Based on the seriousness of the charges against them, I request bail be denied," she said.

"Mr. Whitting?" Judge Street prompted.

Mr. Whitting stood. "My client has no criminal record and is a respected businessman in this community. Denial of bail might cause him and his employees great financial hardship. Based on his longtime social and economic position in Tallulah Falls, I request that a reasonable bail amount be set."

After Mr. Whitting was seated, the judge nodded to Mr. McQuiston.

Mr. McQuiston stood, cleared his throat, and said, "I request the same of my client, please." He sat back down.

I nearly groaned aloud. I didn't know what Sadie was paying this guy, but the best he could do was basically "What he said"? The judge's expression told me he felt the same way.

Judge Street looked at the file again. "A preliminary hearing in this matter will take place on Monday, April 4, at ten thirty a.m. Bail for each defendant is set in the amount of seven hundred fifty thousand dollars."

My jaw dropped, and I slowly turned to look at Sadie.

"It's all right," she said softly. "Mr. Whitting and Mr. McQuiston had already warned that bail would be set high, if at all. We're using a property bond against our house and MacKenzies' Mochas."

Chapter Nine

After the arraignment, I hurried home to get Angus. He and I made it back to the Seven-Year Stitch with only five minutes to spare. I didn't like cutting it that close with regard to opening the shop, but with the busy evening I had scheduled, I knew that if I didn't bring Angus into the shop, he'd be alone all day and most of the night.

I was putting my jacket and purse in my office when I heard the bell over the door jingle. "Be right there!" I called.

When I turned, I was startled to see Todd standing in the office doorway. He'd apparently sprinted from the front door. He bridged the distance between us and pulled me to him in a bear hug. "Aren't you a sight for sore eyes?"

"I'm sorry I didn't come visit you in jail again after Saturday morning," I said.

"Hush and just let me hold you for a minute."

I realized he was slightly trembling. "Are you okay?"

"Not really. I've got a lot on the line right now." He tilted my chin up with his index finger. "Thank you for everything you've done . . . everything you're doing."

"It's nothing. I know you and Blake are innocent, and I intend to help you prove it," I said. "Tell me what happened on Friday night."

Todd released me and stepped out of the office. I followed him to the sit-and-stitch square.

"I'm not sure what happened," he said, sitting on the edge of the sofa facing the window. I perched on the red chair closest to him. "What do you mean, you're not sure?"

"Exactly what I said. And I don't want to talk about it until Blake and I can discuss it alone." Angus came to sit on the floor in front of Todd, and Todd patted his head. "Hey, buddy. How're you doing?"

I was beginning to get frustrated. "Here I am, putting all this effort into helping you prove your innocence, and you won't even tell me what happened? You *are* innocent, aren't you?"

"Yes, Marcy, I am. And I appreciate everything you're doing. I just . . ." He shook his head.

"Do you think Blake is guilty? Do you believe he shot Graham with your gun?" I asked.

"I don't know. Right now I'm doing my best to give Blake the benefit of doubt." He rubbed the back of his neck. "He and I couldn't talk in jail for fear of being overheard. Without talking with him, I honestly don't know what happened."

"Okay."

"Do you believe me?" Todd asked.

I nodded, but there was an unpleasant nagging feeling that made me wonder if his and Blake's conversation would uncover the truth or simply ensure they were telling the same version of events.

He stood. "Come on. Sadie is throwing Blake and me an impromptu celebration for getting out on bail. Let's go have a latte."

"I can't leave the shop," I said. "Congratulate Blake for me, though."

"Sure thing," he said. "Thanks again for your support."

After he left, I realized how drastically his

mood toward me had changed while he was here. When he'd first arrived, he'd been grateful and huggy and warm. When he'd left, he'd been cold. Had he seen the doubt on my face when he asked if I believed him? Because now, I wasn't sure *what* to believe. Despite the fact that he hadn't spoken privately with Blake yet, he could've told me what he saw . . . how he believed the events of Friday night had transpired. Did he not trust me? Was he afraid I'd tell Sadie or Blake something that he'd told me in confidence?

I glanced over at Angus and saw that he was looking apprehensive. He'd felt the vibe of the room change, too. I stood, gave him a kiss on the head, and got him a granola bone to chew on. He took it to his bed beneath the counter. All was now right with his little world. Too bad a tasty treat couldn't turn a person's world around—although hot fudge sundaes could sure make a bad day better.

And rolls. Fresh hot buttery rolls were pure bliss . . . bliss on a bun. Great. I was making myself hungry, and lunch was two hours away.

I glanced out the window and spotted Vera Langhorne heading for the shop. She'd been out of town all last week, and I'd missed her. She—and the crazy stories she undoubtedly had to tell me—would keep my mind off food for a while.

I noticed she was carrying gift bags, so I held the door open for her.

"Hello, darlings," she said, including Angus in her hello. "I bring salutations and souvenirs from Washington." She wore a long-sleeved coral shirt and matching espadrilles with dark denim jeans. She'd had medium blond highlights added to her brown bob, and chunky jewelry completed her casual chic ensemble.

"You look fabulous!" I gave her a quick hug. "Did you have fun?"

"Oh, I had the absolute best time ever. Since it was gals only and we had a suite, we spent most of our time in pj's." She giggled. "Of course, we didn't stay in the suite *all* the time. We visited the spa more than once, tried the various restaurants in and around the hotel, went shopping . . ." She heaved a contented sigh as she sat down in the sit-and-stitch square. "And you remember Paul Samms, the newspaper writer I've been seeing since the masquerade ball?"

I nodded as I took a seat beside her.

"He called me twice last week," she said. "We're having dinner together this evening."

Must be nice, I thought. Here Vera is a widow

in her late fifties to early sixties, and she was having more romantic success than I was. Determined to be happy for her, though, I smiled. "Congratulations. As my grandmother used to say, it sounds like you've got the world by the tail on a downhill pull."

"Things are definitely looking up." She opened the first bag and presented Angus with a Kodiak bear squeak toy.

He took the toy, tossed it into the air, and then pounced on it. Vera and I laughed when the toy let out a loud shriek.

"And this is for you," Vera said, handing me the larger bag.

"Thank you," I said. I opened the bag to find a white spa robe, slippers, and milk chocolate truffles. "Wow, this is wonderful, Vera. I love it."

"I knew you could use some pampering. I didn't realize how badly, though, until I got back home," she said. "I heard there was some trouble at the Brew Crew over the weekend. What happened?"

"That seems to be the million-dollar question," I said. I told her about the shooting, the fact that neither Blake nor Todd seemed willing to divulge what actually happened, and that the men had both been released on bail this morning.

"Are you helping to investigate?" Vera asked. "I mean, after all, you've had your fair share of detective experience since you moved here to Tallulah Falls."

"Please don't remind me. But, yeah, I am doing a little asking around." I lifted and dropped one shoulder. "It's hard to investigate something, though, when the people involved aren't willing to help you."

"I guess it is. Plus, here you are, caught between two men on opposite sides of the law." Vera's face took on a faraway expression like the one I've seen on Mom's face when she's working out the costumes for a movie scene. Undoubtedly, Vera had cast me as "the dame" in some sort of film noir detective story.

"It's really not like that," I said.

Vera's brows shot up, and her expression changed to one of surprise and confusion. "No . . . I guess it's not."

I followed her gaze to the sidewalk outside the shop window. Keira and Todd were walking past, hand in hand. As they strolled by, Todd kept his eyes forward, but Keira turned and raised her free hand in a silly little wave.

I felt like an idiot. Here I was, running all over the place to help prove this guy's innocence, and he was escorting Princess Prisspot down the street. Suddenly, I wanted to just forget about it and turn my back on the whole mess.

But I couldn't do that—Blake and Sadie needed to learn the truth. I only hoped the truth wouldn't be detrimental to them. Anyway, I already had the appointments with Roberto, Mark, and Charles. I couldn't cancel on them now.

"Sweetie, are you okay?" Vera asked gently.

"Never better," I said, forcing a smile. "I'm looking forward to kicking back and enjoying my robe, slippers, and chocolates. Thanks again, Vera. You rock." And on the inside, I told myself one more time that I was perfectly fine with Todd dating Keira and that I didn't need Todd or Ted in my life. But the feeling-sorry-for-myself part of me wanted to devour that entire box of truffles.

I took the gift bag to my office and returned with my Mountmellick embroidery project.

Vera leaned over to see what I was working on. "Ooh, that's pretty. Is it candlewick?"

I explained that it was Mountmellick embroidery, an Irish form of embroidery that—according to the book by Pat Trott, which I had in stock—was introduced in the nineteenth century by Johanna Carter and developed in the town of Mountmellick in county Laoighis.

"The embroidery was used to help women earn money," I said. "The technique uses a lot of different stitches, which could make a good learning tool." That fact had just dawned on me, and Vera saw it in my eyes.

She smiled. "I get the feeling you're thinking about teaching a new class."

"You know, that's not a bad idea."

I was finishing up with a customer when Roberto and his wife, Carla, came into the shop. Angus greeted the newcomers enthusiastically, and they welcomed his attention. As I smiled and told them I'd be with them in a couple of minutes, they moved into the sit-and-stitch square to play ball with Angus.

The customer—an older gentleman who bought a beginner needlepoint kit for his granddaughter—paid and assured me he'd be bringing his wife to the store in a day or two. "She'll love it here. I can't believe she hasn't found your place already."

"Well, I've only been open for a few months," I said.

"That explains it. We spent the winter in Hawaii with our son and his family," he said.

"Now you're making me jealous!" I laughed as I handed him the bag containing the needle-point kit. "I hope your granddaughter enjoys it. And I'll look forward to seeing you again and to meeting your wife."

As the man left, I joined Roberto and Carla in the seating area. "Thanks for your patience . . . and for keeping Angus entertained."

"No problem," Roberto said. "We love dogs."

"It's nice to see you have such a thriving business," Carla said.

Like me, Carla was short and compensated with sky-high heels. She had rich, chestnut-colored hair and green eyes. She seemed as nice as could be, but there was something in her demeanor that suggested she was the final decision-maker in the family.

"May I get you guys something to drink?" I asked. "I have water and sodas in my mini-fridge, and I have hot water for tea and instant cappuccino."

"No, thank you. We just had lunch," Carla said.

"Yeah, I'm fine," said Roberto.

Angus, tired from the recent romping, took his new squeak toy and loped over to lie down by the window.

Roberto looked around at the dolls I'd dressed in elaborately embroidered outfits. "You made these clothes?"

"I did." I sat on the chair nearest the counter. "Although my mom is, of course, the expert, I can do some costuming myself. What types of films do you make?"

"We do all kinds," Roberto said. "We do small-budget indie films mostly, some documentaries."

"We do horror, drama, action, coming-of-age," Carla chimed in. "We had a film debut at Sundance last year. It was called *Wicker*."

"I've been wanting to see that!" And I had . . . ever since I'd Googled Roberto's company and learned they'd done the film. Until then, I'd never heard of it. It was about a woman who overcame financial hardship following her husband's tragic death. The woman supported herself, her children, and her invalid mother by making wicker baskets.

"It's based on a true story," Carla said.

And there was my opening. "Speaking of true stories, maybe someone will make a screenplay based on the murder of Graham Stott. I attended the arraignment before coming to work this morning. Isn't this whole thing a nightmare?"

"Yes, it is." Roberto cast a weary sidelong glance at his wife.

"I warned Roberto not to go to that stupid party," Carla said. "I knew there would be trouble."

I leaned closer. "How did you know?"

"Because that group can't get together *sober* without fighting," she said. "A party at a bar was simply throwing gasoline on an open flame."

"Graham was overall a good guy," Roberto said. "But he almost always wound up acting like a jerk when more than a couple of us got together."

"If no one really liked Graham and he was known for his bad behavior at these types of events, then why did Todd invite him?" I asked.

"He pretty much had to." Roberto inclined his head. "Graham loaned Todd some of the money to get the Brew Crew off the ground."

"So Todd and Graham were pretty close friends, then," I said.

Roberto barked out a laugh. "Hardly. I don't know of anyone who was all that close to Graham. It's just that he and his family have always had money to burn. Whenever anybody needed money, they knew where to go."

"Thank goodness we never had to stoop that low," Carla said, although I noticed that Roberto averted his gaze.

"Roberto, while we're on the subject of Graham and the Alpha Sigs, may I ask you a question?" I asked.

He briefly looked back at me, but he still appeared to be uncomfortable. "I guess so."

"Did Blake ever date Tawny Milligan?" I asked. "Somebody was talking about her and mentioned that she'd dated several of the fraternity brothers. Since Sadie and I are best friends, I wanted to know if there's anything I should avoid talking with her about. She told me she didn't really know Tawny."

"I don't know if she and Blake dated or not," Roberto said.

"Puh-leeze," Carla said. "That little tramp dated any of the Alpha Sigs she could dig her long fake fingernails into, including Blake MacKenzie. I met Tawny our first semester in college. We were friends before I started dating Roberto."

"It doesn't sound like the two of you are friends anymore," I said.

Carla shook her head vehemently. "Oh, no. That so-called friendship fell flat on its face when Tawny tried to steal Roberto away from

me. As if!" She took her husband's arm posses-
sively. "After that, she moved on to the other
Alpha Sigs. If you ask me, she was trying to
snag a rich man to take care of her."

"Did she?" I asked.

"Who knows?" Carla huffed. "She was with
a different guy every time you saw her. She ru-
ined her reputation. I heard that after college
she even changed her name to try to escape her
sordid past."

"She changed her name?" That would certainly explain why I'd been unable to find a
recent phone listing for Tawny Milligan. "That's
extreme. Who did she become?"

Carla shrugged. "I have no idea. I guess she
wanted to start over, and she wanted to do so
without people who knew the truth about her
exposing her as a fraud."

"Maybe she really had changed," I said.

"Maybe, but I doubt it," Carla said. "I think
she had to have had a very compelling reason
to go incognito."

"What do you think it was?" I asked.

"I've always thought she hit the mother
lode, you know?" Carla leaned her head back
against the sofa and looked up at the ceiling as
she spun her tale. "I think she met some fancy-
schmancy guy with a lot of money and clout.

Together they came up with a new identity for Tawny so his family would accept her. She changed her name, turned her back on her past—along with everyone she ever knew—and she started living this new life."

"That's good," I said. "Do you think you'd recognize her if you ever saw her again?"

Carla raised her head. "Oh, sure I would. I'd know her anywhere. No amount of plastic surgery could hide those violet eyes, and she was too vain about them to cover them up with contact lenses. She loved having eyes like Elizabeth Taylor's."

Roberto looked at his watch and then at his wife. "Babe, we need to talk about costuming. It *is* what we're here for."

"You're right." She gave me a half smile. "You have to forgive me. I tend to go off on tangents."

"That's okay. I do it, too," I said.

Before Carla and I could go off on a tangent about going off on tangents, Roberto explained that for their current project they would need Depression-era costumes, furniture, and props. "Are you familiar with Madeleine Vionnet?"

"I know she's famous for bringing the cross-cut bias method to the fashion world," I said.

"Mom has done more gangster films than you can imagine."

"That's the type of elegant look we're going for," Carla said.

"We'll also need some glass and dinnerware pieces from that era," said Roberto. "Do you know where we can find those?"

"This sounds like a huge project, and I'm afraid I couldn't do you justice." I stood and walked over to the counter. I wrote Mom's office number on the back of a Seven-Year Stitch business card and took the card back over to Roberto. "Here. Call Mom. She'll put you in touch with someone who'll do a fantastic job for you."

Roberto and Carla were delighted, and my conscience was a little less burdened for deceiving them about my own costuming skills . . . or lack thereof.

Chapter Ten

As soon as Roberto and Carla left, I called Sadie to tell her about their visit. "They—or, rather, Roberto—didn't have much to say about what happened Friday night, but Carla had plenty to say about Tawny Milligan," I told her. "She and Tawny were friends before Tawny tried to move in on Roberto."

"I can see where that would definitely put the brakes on a friendship," Sadie said.

"Get this: Carla said that Tawny's reputation was so bad by the time she graduated from college that she changed her name. Or, at least, that's what Carla heard."

"Which would explain why you couldn't find her in the white pages." Sadie's statement mirrored my earlier thought. "I'll ask Blake if he remembers her or knows anything about her. I don't see why she'd be all that important to finding out who shot Graham, though. I mean, she wasn't even at the Brew Crew Friday night, was she?"

"I don't think so. But I still believe she could tell us something important . . . maybe something about who might've had it in for Graham. I'd just really like to talk with her," I told Sadie.

"Well, like I said, I'll talk with Blake and see what he says about her."

"Thanks," I said, hoping desperately that Blake hadn't been one of the guys who'd dated Tawny. "After work, I'm meeting with Mark, the personal trainer. And after that, I'm driving to McMinnville to talk with Charles."

"Wow. You've got a busy night ahead of you. Blake and I appreciate everything you're doing for us," said Sadie. "And, of course, Todd does too."

"Uh, yeah. . . . By the way, I saw Todd strolling down the street hand in hand with Keira."

"They were holding hands?" she asked.

"Mm-hmm. And that's fine," I added quickly. "That's great. I'm glad they worked out their differences or whatever."

"I heard Keira ask Todd to do her a favor. Maybe she was taking him . . ." I could tell Sadie was struggling to come up with a suitable favor. ". . . to look at her car or something. Todd is pretty handy with vehicles."

"Sadie, it's okay. I guess Todd and I weren't meant to be." I gave a short laugh. "I'm beginning to think Angus O'Ruff is the only guy destined to be in my life . . . at least, for the time being."

At the sound of his name, Angus lifted his head, cocked it comically to the side, and then flopped it back down with an exaggerated sigh.

Terrific. Even my dog was depressed about my state of affairs—or lack of affairs.

"Since you've got to do so much this evening, and you're doing it for Blake, Todd, and me, why don't you let me bring you a chicken salad croissant about half an hour before you close up shop?" she asked.

"That would be great," I said. "Thanks."

"And while I'm there, I can take Angus on home for you and feed him. That way, you'll have one less thing to worry about," she said, reminding me that she had a key to my house.

I'd given her the key when I first moved to Tallulah Falls for safekeeping in case I ever locked myself out . . . or died inside my house. Sadie or Blake could come to check on me if no one saw me out and about for a couple of days.

Have I mentioned that my imagination some-times borders on the macabre?

"You've got plenty of your own stuff to oc-cupy you," I said. "It won't take me that much extra time to get Angus settled."

"Let me do this for you, Marce. It's the least I can do."

"All right." Maybe she felt the need to do me a favor, since I was helping out with the investigation. She didn't need to do anything, but maybe she thought she did. "Thanks."

"I'll see you in a bit," she said.

Ending the call, I couldn't help but wonder—knowing Sadie like I did—just what she had up her sleeve.

The afternoon was zipping along. Several cus-tomers had been in—some to browse, some to buy. The latest had bought a set of tapestry needles she planned to use in an attempt to mend the upholstery of an antique chair. I wished her luck, but I was thinking she'd be better off taking the chair to a professional. She was more adventurous than I am. But then, I've never been big on upholstery mending.

The bells over the shop door jingled. Lost in my reverie, I half expected it to be the customer coming back to return the tapestry needles because she'd decided to hire out the job. Instead, it was Ted.

"Earth to Marcy," he said, grinning at the bemused expression on my face. "Are you in there?"

I smiled. "Yes. I'm here. Hello."

Angus loped over to greet Ted and to show him his new toy.

"What've you got there, Angus?" Ted asked. "A bear?"

"Yeah," I said. "Vera brought it to him from Washington." I jerked my head toward the sit-and-stitch square. "Let's have a seat."

He accompanied me to the sofa facing the window. "You appeared to be lost in thought when I walked in. What was on your mind?"

"Upholstery, believe it or not."

Angus lay down near us and busied himself with making the bear squeak.

"Strange thing to be mulling over, I guess. But I prefer it to what I expected you to say." He smiled at me, and I was struck by how strong and handsome he was. The pale blue dress shirt he wore today complemented his eyes, and a sexy half smile was playing about his lips.

"And what did you expect me to say?" I asked.

"That you were thinking about Graham Stott's murder."

"At least one of us was right," I said with a grin. "Because that's *exactly* what I expected you to say."

"Has Todd, Blake, or Sadie confided anything to you about Friday night?"

I shook my head. "I'm as much in the dark as anyone else. I do have a theory, though."

"Naturally," he said. "Let's hear it, Inch-High."

Inch-High. Short for Inch-High Private Eye. It wasn't *beautiful* or *sweetheart*, but it was something. I was glad he was relaxed enough today to joke with me.

"One, I believe both Blake and Todd are innocent but that neither knows for sure what happened and isn't a hundred percent convinced the other one didn't pull the trigger," I said. "But I think the shooter killed Graham and then ran into the bathroom beside the room where Graham was shot."

Ted pursed his lips. "Let me get this straight. The killer—unseen by either MacKenzie or Calloway—uses Calloway's gun to shoot Graham Stott. He then tosses the gun onto the floor—still unseen—and goes and hides in the bathroom."

"When you put it like that, it sounds ridiculous."

"Isn't that what you told me?" he asked, struggling to avoid laughing.

"I said nothing about anyone tossing a gun around," I said. "That would be stupid."

"Yeah, it could go off and kill somebody." This time, he did laugh.

"Are you positive the gun found in the room was the one used to shoot Graham Stott?" I asked.

"The victim was shot with a .38 caliber revolver," Ted said. "The gun in the room was a .38 revolver—Calloway's .38 revolver."

"But has a ballistics test been done?"

He smiled. "You watch too many detective shows, you know that? We need to get you interested in something else."

"Has it been done?" I asked.

"The major crime team is working on it, but I don't have a report on it yet," he said.

"So the gun found in the room has not been positively identified as the murder weapon." I steepled my fingers.

"There's a chance it isn't the murder weapon, Counselor, but it's a very slim chance," Ted said. "What are the odds that Calloway and the killer had the same type of gun?"

"Blake has the same type of gun as Todd." I regretted those words as soon as I uttered them. "What I mean is that .38 revolvers are common . . . especially around here. I learned that not long after I came to Tallulah Falls."

He draped an arm around my shoulders. "Believe me, I understand how you must be feeling. But please leave this case to the professionals. Don't go playing Nancy Drew."

"I'm not . . . not really," I said. "It's just hard. Sadie has been my best friend since we were in college, and Blake treats me like a little sister."

"I know, Marce, and I truly feel for you. But I don't want you to get hurt . . . physically or emotionally," he said. "Some of our best people are on this case. We'll get to the truth."

"I know you will," I said with a smile.

"Are you free for dinner tonight?"

"I'm afraid not. I've got an appointment with a personal trainer to learn some exercises to build strength in my arms." I flexed the muscles in my right arm to show him how puny they were.

"What on earth for?" he asked. "Your arms look great."

"Maybe so, but I'm tired of having so much trouble lifting and carrying boxes of supplies. And the damsel-in-distress role is becoming tiresome."

"You can always call on me, damsel," Ted said. "I don't care what you're wearing—dis dress, dat dress, jeans . . ."

I threw my head back against the sofa cushion and groaned. "Worst pun ever!" I laughed. "I'm happy to see you in better spirits today, though."

"I'm happy Manu will be back at the end of the week," he said. "So can I get a rain check on dinner?"

"You bet."

I looked at the clock and decided that if no one else came in this afternoon, I had a good forty-five minutes to devote to my Mountmellick project. That should be enough time to finish a shamrock or two. Or, at least, one and a half.

I'd just started making progress when Mom called. She wanted to know, "Who are Roberto and Carla Gutierrez, and why did you ask them to call me?"

"I meant to phone and explain all that to you, but this afternoon has been crazy," I said. "Roberto was one of the guys at Todd's party Friday night."

"The party where the man was shot, I'm guessing," she said.

"Right," I said. "Anyway, I was trying to

think of a way to talk with him without being obvious that I wanted to talk about the murder. Since he and his wife make indie films, I told them I was your daughter and was interested in making costumes for them."

"You little liar!"

"But I *am* your daughter," I protested.

"Whatever happened to *I hate throwing your name around* and *I refuse to ride on my mother's coattails*?" Mom asked.

"Desperate times, Mom. Desperate times."

"Did you find out anything?"

"Not much about what happened Friday night," I said. "But I did learn that this couple adores you and thinks you're an artistic genius."

She gave a throaty chuckle. "I do love people of quality."

"I'm not kidding, Mom. They were familiar with all of your better-known—and many of your lesser-known—films."

"So, did you sign on to make the costumes for them?"

"Are you kidding? You know better than that," I said. "They said they're working on a Depression-era piece, and I told them I was afraid I couldn't do the film justice. I said that you, however, might know someone in the Seattle area who could do a terrific job on the project."

"You know what? You're right. I do." She laughed again. "I'll give the Gutierrezes a call and see if they're as knowledgeable about me as you say they are. And I'll tell them about my friend in Seattle."

"Thanks, Mom. I owe you one."

"You owe me *thousands*," she said. "I've simply never cashed in. So, what's up with Todd and Ted?"

"Todd and Keira, the girl he took to the ball last month, are apparently at the hand-holding stage," I said. "Ted did ask me to dinner this evening, but I can't go because I have an appointment with a personal trainer."

"A personal trainer?" she asked.

"Yep. It'll probably just be the one visit, though."

"For the record, I'm Team Edward," she said, referring to the debate among *Twilight* fans over whether the heroine should choose the vampire or the werewolf.

"And I'm Team Jacob," I said with a giggle.

"This trainer . . . was he at the party Friday night?" she asked.

"Uh-huh." She knew me so well.

"Be careful, love. I don't like you getting involved with all this mayhem and intrigue."

"That's your world, Mom, not mine. And

I'm planning on shelving my deerstalker and magnifying glass and leaving the crime solving to the professionals after tonight."

Todd came in, and I held up an index finger to let him know I'd be with him in a second. Angus got up and greeted him. That dog was the best helper ever. He even outshone Jill.

"I've got to go, Mom. Someone just walked in. I'll talk with you soon." I told her I loved her and ended the call.

"Hi," Todd said.

"Hi, yourself," I said.

"Sadie sent me to get Angus for her. She said she'd have the croissant ready when I get back with him."

"I suppose she was too busy to come get him herself?" I asked.

"Something like that." He shoved his hands into the pockets of his well-worn jeans. "She told me you saw Keira and me walking down the street this morning."

"Uh, yeah. I'd have had to have been blind to miss it," I said. "You didn't see Keira wave to me?"

"No. I wasn't paying attention. I was trying to hurry up and . . ."

When he trailed off, I resumed my stitching. "It's not a big deal."

He took his hands from his pockets and came to sit on the ottoman in front of me. "It's a big deal if you have the wrong impression about Keira and me." He took my shoulders so I'd be compelled to look into those soulful chocolate eyes of his. "She asked me to do her a favor. She said this guy she used to date has been hassling her. He saw us together at the masquerade ball, so she wanted him to think we were a couple so he'd leave her alone."

Oh, sure. And the guy just happened *to be in such close proximity to my shop that Keira needed to parade Todd by my window so she could give her gloating little wave? Riiight. Do you honestly believe that, Todd?* That's what I thought. What I actually said was, "Again, it's not a big deal."

"Then why do I feel like it is?" he asked.

I shrugged.

"That!" He spread his hands. "That little—" He imitated my shrug . . . rather clumsily, if you asked me. "That speaks volumes."

"Good," I said. "Then I shouldn't have to say anything else."

"Will you please cut me some slack? I've had a pretty rough seventy-two hours," he said.

I put aside my embroidery project, stood, and put some distance between Todd and me.

"I realize that. I, on the other hand, have had a glorious time trying to figure out what happened Friday night and to prove your innocence. Adding to all my fun is the fact that you won't even share your version of events with me so I can compare it to what I've learned from the others I've spoken with. You're too busy walking up and down the street in front of my window with your girlfriend!"

"See?" Todd jumped up from the ottoman. "I *knew* that bothered you!"

"Do you want to know what bothers me? I'll tell you what genuinely irks me to the core: the fact that on Friday, before the shooting, you told me we needed to talk about *things*. I thought one of these *things* you wanted to talk about was whether we could have a relationship. This morning, you couldn't trust me enough to tell me what happened after I left the pub." My eyes filled, and I turned away, hoping Todd hadn't seen my tears. "I think that answers the relationship question fairly succinctly. Don't you?"

"Marcy." He bridged the distance between us and put his hand on my back.

I moved away from his touch. "Please tell Sadie I've changed my mind. I'm locking up the shop now and taking Angus home after all."

Chapter Eleven

Since I cried all the way home, I had to wash my face and redo my makeup as soon as I got there. I felt betrayed . . . not only by Todd, but by Sadie and Blake as well. And I didn't feel that Todd had betrayed me with Keira. He and I weren't a couple. I might've felt a sting of jealousy when I first saw them together, but I didn't feel betrayed. What I was so hurt by was the fact that no one trusted me enough to tell me what happened—or even what they *thought* happened—on Friday night.

I put Angus, his food, water, and new squeaky bear outside on the back porch. It wasn't supposed to rain tonight, but if it did, he could doze on the porch swing. I didn't have time for dinner, so I grabbed a protein bar on the way out the door.

My phone rang as I was en route to the Jeep. It saw that it was Sadie, and I let the call go to voice mail.

Mark's gym was only about a fifteen-minute drive from Tallulah Falls. It was named, simply enough, Mark's Gym. Even from the outside, I could tell this was a man's gym and that it wasn't used to catering to women at all. There was no landscaping to speak of. Although there was mulch on either side of the sidewalk and in front of the building, there were no plants. A concrete planter near the door contained only sand, cigarette butts, and gum wrappers.

I wiped my damp palms down the sides of my jeans before opening the door and stepping inside. To my left was a boxing ring where two men whose hands were taped and who were wearing headgear were sparring. Beyond the boxing ring, punching bags of various sizes, shapes, and colors hung from the ceiling. To my right, there were all kinds of free weights and aerobic machines, such as ellipticals, treadmills, rowing machines, and cycles. Huge, muscular men stopped what they were doing to turn and stare at me. I had never felt so tiny in all my life . . . and that was saying something.

I raised my right hand in greeting. "Hi. I have an appointment with Mark."

An older, scraggly-bearded gentleman who was watching the sparring match bellowed, "Mark!"

Mark immediately poked his head out of a doorway to the far left of the gym. "Hey, Marcy, come on back. Guys, you can put your eyes back in your head and close your mouths now."

I walked past the boxing ring and punching bags where Mark waited to usher me into his office. The room was large and sparsely furnished. In one corner was a black metal desk with an uncomfortable-looking chair and a gray filing cabinet. A calculator and a laptop sat on the desk. In the other corner was a pyramid of free weights. The only other items in the room were a leather sofa and a flat-screen television, which were on opposite sides of the room. The rest of the office was wide-open space.

Mark pushed the door closed behind me. "As you can probably tell, we don't have many female members. Because of that, I couldn't find any dumbbells around here lighter than ten pounds." He reached into a deep drawer of the desk and brought out two water bottles. "For today, these will have to suffice as your weights."

I was glad to see that Mark had dropped the condescending attitude he'd adopted over the phone. Apparently, he'd decided my interest in him was professional after all.

I smiled and picked up the water bottles. "These are going to make me stronger?"

"No. After you leave here, I want you to go to a sporting goods store and buy two three pound dumbbells," he said. "When those stop being a challenge, I want you to go up to five-pound weights."

"Okay." This man was serious about his job. And given his good looks, women would likely beat a path to his door for personal training if they knew about him. "Why don't you advertise? I'd never even have known about this place if I hadn't met you Friday night."

"I enjoy doing what I'm doing. Contrary to what anyone else thinks, I don't feel the need to expand my business."

"I'm sorry," I said, surprised by the sharpness of his tone. "I wasn't suggesting that at all."

"I know," he said. "And I apologize for being rude. I've just heard that spiel about growing my business a lot lately, and it's become a touchy subject."

"I understand. I don't think you're the only one who feels bigger isn't necessarily better," I said. "If I'm not mistaken, Blake had to make that clear to Graham Stott on Friday."

Mark frowned. "Graham wanted Blake to expand?"

"From what I understand, he wanted Blake to begin franchising." I shook my head. "Which is kinda goofy, if you ask me. How could a small, independent coffeehouse compete with Starbucks?"

"And why would Blake want to try to compete and lose the charm of MacKenzies' Mochas?" Mark asked. "I don't know why Graham thought we should all become business tycoons."

"Maybe it was because he cared about all of you and that's how he showed it—by trying to make sure you were financially secure," I said.

"Graham might've been financially secure, but he was one of the most unhappy people I've ever known."

I frowned. "How come?"

"Who knows? It always seemed to me like he had everything from a material standpoint but nothing that really mattered," said Mark. "He was rather sad in that respect." He took a deep breath. "But you aren't here to chitchat. Let's get down to business."

Using the two water bottles as dumbbells, Mark showed me how to do biceps curls, rotational dumbbell arm curls, triceps overhead extensions, and triceps kickbacks.

"I want you to start out with three sets of twelve repetitions," he said. "Did you tell me your shop is across the street from the Brew Crew?"

I nodded.

"Is it all right if I stop in within the next day or so to see how you're doing? I'd like to check your form with your actual dumbbells."

"That sounds great, Mark. Thanks." As I was writing him a check for our session, I asked if he'd known Blake and Todd before they went to college together.

"I'm afraid I've known those two clowns pretty much all my life," he said with a laugh. "We started kindergarten together."

"Do you think it's possible that either of them shot Graham?" I asked.

He sighed. "It's hard for me to believe that one of them did, but I've come to realize over the years that people snap sometimes and do things they could never have imagined doing in a normal situation." He accepted my check and placed it in the top desk drawer. "Do you need a receipt, Marcy?"

"No," I said. "I get what you're saying about people snapping, but *murder*? That's a pretty extreme snap."

"It was an extreme night," Mark said. "And Todd and Blake can both be quick-tempered when provoked. Once, at a high school dance, some guy poured punch all down the front of Blake's cousin's dress."

"On purpose?" I asked.

"Yeah. The cousin—Missy—had been dating the guy, but she broke things off with him. So he decided to humiliate her in front of everybody."

"That's terrible! What a jerk," I said.

"Blake wasn't able to get to the front of the gym in time to prevent the guy from upending the punch bowl on Missy, but he did break the guy's nose. He might've done worse if the principal hadn't pulled him off the guy." Mark went over and opened the door for me, effectively indicating that our time was up. "All I'm saying is that you never know anybody as well as you think you do. For instance, a few months ago, my wife took off." He shook his

THE LONG STITCH GOOD NIGHT

head slowly as though still in disbelief. "And I thought we were solid, you know? I was attentive, I listened to her, I gave her presents, I picked up after myself. . . . I don't know where I went wrong."

"One day, she'll realize what she gave up," I said. "And she'll be sorry."

He smiled slightly. "I think she might be sorry already."

As I stepped into the hallway, I realized I'd forgotten to ask Mark about Tawny Milligan. But he'd already closed the door behind me, and it would seem odd to go back just to ask him if he remembered her. Besides, I could ask about her when he came by the shop to check out my dumbbell form.

Before starting the drive to McMinnville, I called Reggie. She answered on the first ring, and I put my phone on speaker before backing out of the gym's parking lot.

"Ted told me Manu is coming home at the end of the week," I said. "What great news."

"Thanks. I'm thrilled," she said. "I've missed him like crazy. By the way, have you seen Riley's baby yet?"

"I have. I went by the hospital Saturday. Have you?"

"Yeah. I stopped in yesterday. Isn't she precious?" Reggie asked.

"Adorable. Were you at the arraignment this morning?" I hadn't seen Reggie there, but the courtroom had been fairly packed, so it was possible I'd overlooked her.

"No, I had to be at the library at eight thirty. I heard that the boys made bail, though, so that's good," she said.

"Reggie, why won't they talk about what occurred on the night Graham was shot? They won't tell me anything . . . none of them—not even Sadie. They won't even give me a clue as to what happened. Why don't they trust me?"

"*Mitra*, you can't take it personally," she said gently. "Many attorneys instruct their clients not to divulge details about a case to anyone, including their closest friends."

"I know, but it sure feels like a slight." I hoped that didn't sound immature.

"Look at it this way: If you know something and are called to testify, you have to tell what you know," said Reggie. "Spouses are different because of the marital communications privilege, which would explain why Sadie hasn't told you what Blake might've confided to her."

"I guess that makes sense. Let me ask you one other thing before I let you go." I told her about Tawny Milligan, her sullied reputation, and her possible name change.

"And you feel this woman could be important to Graham's murder investigation?" she asked.

"Well, I think she could at least speak with the defense attorneys about the dynamics at play among the men and possibly provide them with another viable suspect."

"All right. I know a few folks at OSU," she said. "I'll give them a call tomorrow and see what I can do about helping you track down Miss Milligan."

"Thank you, Reggie. I appreciate that."

I was glad the restaurant bar where Charles and I had agreed to meet wasn't crowded. Of course, it *was* Monday evening, but it was nice not to have to search through a throng of people to find him. He was sitting at the end of the bar watching a basketball game and drinking from a longneck.

Charles wasn't the best-looking guy I'd ever seen, but he wasn't unattractive either. He just didn't seem to care much about his appearance. His shirttail was half in and half out of his pants, there was a large mustard stain on his tie, and he looked as if he might've forgotten to comb his hair this morning . . . and possibly *yesterday* morning as well.

"Hi." I took a seat on the stool beside him.

"Hey, there. Want a beer?" he asked. "It's dollar longneck night."

"No, thanks," I said with a smile. "I'd love a water, though."

"How about a limeade?" He took a swig of his beer. "They make great ones here."

"Okay. A limeade it is."

Charles signaled the bartender and ordered my drink and another longneck. "You'll like the limeade," he told me. "Not too tart, not too sweet."

"I wasn't expecting you to be so familiar with this place," I said. "It's quite a drive from Portland."

"It is, but it's a nice halfway spot between Portland and the coast . . . among other areas. I sometimes meet sources here," he said. "So, did you attend the arraignment?"

"I did." I gave Charles the details of the hearing.

"I'm surprised the judge granted bail." He didn't look up from the notes he was scribbling. "Who sat the bench?"

"It was Judge Street. Both defense attorneys

spoke about the men's ties to the community, their businesses, and the financial hardships they'd suffer if denied bail," I said.

"Very good." He finally put down his nubby, chewed-on pencil and looked at me. "Anything else you can tell me?"

"I'm afraid not. I'd hoped to dig up more background information on Graham and any enemies he might have had, but I've not had much luck doing so." I sighed. "It seems the woman in the best position to provide that information has disappeared."

"Really? Who's that?" he asked.

"Tawny Milligan," I said.

Charles's expression froze. Before he could speak, the bartender placed my drink in front of me and put another beer in front of Charles.

"Thank you," I said, handing the man a five-dollar bill. I turned back to Charles, who was downing the rest of his first longneck with a trembling hand. "So, did you know her?"

"I knew her," he said. "She was a sweet girl. She didn't deserve to have her name dragged through the mud the way it was. That—" He broke off, staring at some point in the distance, his head turned toward but looking beyond me, his eyes seeing nothing except maybe a memory of Tawny Milligan.

I wondered if she'd had Charles fooled the way Keira was apparently able to trick or manipulate Todd. What did this Tawny chick have over all these fraternity guys? Was she the most gorgeous woman they'd ever seen? Was she like Snow White, and the fraternity brothers were the seven dopes? I suddenly imagined the fairy-tale princess in denim cutoffs and a halter top, singing while she and forest creatures cleaned the frat house and did the laundry.

"What happened to Tawny after graduation?" I asked.

With some effort, Charles shook off his haze and gave me his attention. "It's like you said. She disappeared. It's the way she wanted it. She wanted a fresh start." He smiled faintly. "We all want that sometimes, don't we?"

"Of course we do, but we know we can't have it," I said. "Do you have any idea where she went?"

Charles frowned and looked down at his thumbnail.

"Did she change her name?" I asked, determined to get some sort of answer, even if it was an *I don't know*.

Unfortunately, before Charles could—or would—say anything, his phone rang. And I swear he looked relieved. "Excuse me." He answered the call. "Hey, buddy. What's up?" He grinned as he listened to the caller's response. "I'm finishing up my meeting right now, and I'll be home in a little over an hour. Do you need me to bring you anything?" He winked at me, as if I were somehow a party to the call or in cahoots with him on something. "All right, then. I love you, son. See you in a bit." He ended the call.

"How old is he?" I asked.

"Nine . . . almost ten. He's a handful, but he's my life," he said. "You got any kids?"

"No. Is he your only child?"

Charles nodded. "His mother and I discussed having another one . . . but she isn't with us anymore."

"I'm sorry to hear that," I said.

"My sister is at my house with him now, and I really need to get home," he said. "Thank you for meeting with me and keeping me posted on this murder investigation. It's kind of hard to swallow, hitting so close to home and all. . . . But that's another reason I want to keep up with it—not only for the paper, but for myself."

"I understand completely."

He pursed his lips as he put his nubby pencil into his shirt pocket. "I gotta ask again, though, Marcy, what are you hoping to get out of this? And don't give me the song and dance about wanting to help your friends. You want me to give you credit in the article? Do you want to share the byline? What's your angle?"

"I don't know that I'd call it an angle," I said, deciding to ask for something in return rather than telling him I was only after the truth and that it wasn't a *song and dance*. A man who'd already decided everyone had an angle had already proved he wouldn't buy that story. "I sure would love it if you could mention the Seven-Year Stitch in any articles your paper does on places of interest on the coast or in Tallulah Falls."

"That's it? That's all you want?" he asked incredulously.

"That's it." I smiled. "My shop is fairly new, and I could use the publicity. I don't have a large advertising budget, so this could be huge for me."

"Fair enough! I'll even do a story designed to showcase the shop in the big Memorial Day issue," he said. "How's that?"

"That would be fantastic." It really would. Sadie had told me that during the summer— starting with Memorial Day weekend—the shopping complex would get a lot of tourists from up north as people traveled to the coast or on to California on vacation.

"Great." He slid off the bar stool and patted me on the shoulder. "I'll be in touch."

When Charles left, I finished drinking my limeade and wondered how weird it was that two of the fraternity brothers' marriages had apparently crumbled. And I'd talked with both men tonight. Was it merely statistics or was there more to it? I also thought about the reactions I got every time I brought up the name Tawny Milligan. It was time to throw that name out to Blake and Todd and watch their reactions.

Chapter Twelve

On my way home from McMinnville the night before, I'd stopped at a twenty-four-hour supercenter and bought a set of three-pound dumbbells. They were purple with a swirly design painted on them in silver. They were cute and chic, which made it more likely that I'd actually use them.

I let Angus into the shop and then ran back out to the Jeep to get the tote containing my dumbbells and the Mountmellick project. Since Angus was quick to settle in with a chew treat, I decided to put my things in my office and go through a few of my arm exercises.

I'd finished my biceps curls and was into my second set of triceps kickbacks when the bells over the door jingled. "Welcome to the Seven-Year Stitch," I called. "I'll be right out."

"Take your time," Reggie shouted back.

I could hear her playing with Angus, so I hurried through the rest of the set before stepping out of my office.

Reggie whirled around as I entered the shop, her pale green tunic floating around her waist prettily. Her dark eyes narrowed behind her round wire-rimmed glasses. "You look flushed. What were you doing back there?"

"Arm exercises. I'm tired of being such a noodle-armed weakling."

"Okay," she said with a grin. "I'll keep my noodle arms. I came by to tell you I heard from my friend at OSU."

"Did she know anything about Tawny?" I asked, sitting on the sofa facing the window.

Reggie sat on the other sofa so we could look at each other while we were talking. "She remembered Tawny well because Tawny had worked for her. You see, my friend is a division secretary, and every year a couple of students assist her as part of a work-study-type program. It's part of a financial aid package."

"And Tawny was part of this work-study program?" I asked.

Reggie nodded. "Carol said Tawny was a real hardship case but a capable and determined young woman. Not only was she part of the school's work-study program, Tawny cleaned, did odd jobs—including tutoring—for other students, and held down a part-time job at a restaurant on campus."

"When did she have time to study . . . much less get a bad reputation?"

"I have no idea," Reggie said. "But Carol told me Tawny graduated with honors."

"What field was she going into?" I asked.

"She got her bachelor's degree in human resources."

I frowned. "It doesn't make sense that she'd change her name. Wouldn't she want all those accolades and employer references to follow her into her career?"

"A name change wouldn't cause her to lose any of that," said Reggie. "When a woman marries, she usually takes her husband's surname. Then when the woman gets her transcripts or when she requests letters of recommendation, she simply reminds whomever she's speaking with of the name she previously used."

"Duh," I said, smacking myself on the forehead. "I knew that, of course. I just wasn't thinking. I've even seen a space on job applications for would-be employees to put any *formerly known as* names."

"Right. And it wouldn't raise eyebrows much at all if she kept *Tawny* as a middle name," Reggie said. "Anyway, my friend said she'll look into it further and let me know—hopefully, later today—any current information she's able to dig up on Tawny Milligan. Carol also said that if she can find a working number for the woman, she'll see if Tawny would be willing to talk with defense attorneys in the case."

"That's great. Thanks so much, Reggie."

"I don't know how much it would help matters, but it would at least satisfy your curiosity," she said with a grin.

A woman who looked to be in her early to mid-seventies entered the shop. She had tight reddish brown curls and wore red-framed glasses. Her elfin figure was swallowed up in a scarlet sweater dress.

"Good morning," I said.

"Hello." She waved absently to Reggie and me as she approached the counter, where Jill the mannequin stood guard. "I need eight skeins of white angora yarn, young lady."

My eyes widened, and Reggie covered her mouth with her hand. I rushed over to the counter, thinking it was time the lady got a stronger prescription for those red glasses. Reggie said she needed to get back to the library and scrambled out the door.

"Did you say you need eight skeins?" I asked.

"Yes, dear. I'm going to crochet an afghan for my niece. She's getting married in June." She looked at Jill, trying to include her in the conversation. You couldn't accuse Ms. Magoo here of being rude. "I'm using an intricate old pattern. It was my grandmother's."

"I'm sure the afghan will be lovely," I said. "Would you like to take a seat while I get your yarn?"

"Oh, no, thank you," she said. "I'm fine right here."

I decided to take the eight skeins of white angora from the storeroom rather than the yarn bins. I gathered the yarn and noted that my supply was nearly wiped out. I made a mental note to order more this afternoon. When I returned, the customer was squinting at the mannequin.

"Here you are," I said brightly. "Will you need some hooks or anything else?"

"No." She plucked one of the skeins of yarn out of my arms and inspected it carefully. "This will do very well." She lowered her voice. "The girl behind the counter . . . is she new?"

Not sure what else to do, I nodded.

"I thought so. She's a little shy, isn't she?"

Again I nodded. I thought fleetingly of saying that Jill couldn't talk, but I decided that was unnecessary. If the woman ever realized her faux pas, she'd think I was being supercilious.

I rang up the customer's yarn and placed it in a large periwinkle Seven-Year Stitch bag. I took an embroidery class flyer and placed that in the bag as well. Handing the bag to the customer, I said, "Thank you so much for shopping with us. I hope you have a terrific day."

"You, too." She lifted a hand in Jill's direction. "Hang in there, honey. You'll get a feel for things in no time." She gave me a little nod and left.

Grinning, I put my arm around Jill's shoulders. "Yeah, kid. You'll catch on."

Mom called around lunchtime. She'd spoken with Carla and Roberto and had given them her friend's contact information in Seattle.

"You were absolutely right, Marcella. I believe they really are fans of my work."

"Told you so," I said in a singsong voice.

"It was truly gratifying to have my work appreciated by someone who doesn't know me . . . who doesn't have any sort of stake in things," she said. "By the way, while I had them on the line, I did a little snooping of my own."

"What did you do?" I asked, half dreading her answer.

"I told Carla and Roberto that I'm concerned about you. I said that you hadn't lived in Tallulah Falls for all that long, and now two of your friends are facing murder convictions." She gave her usual throaty chuckle. "I made it sound as if I was terrified that you'd moved to Oregon and fallen in with a gang of ruffians."

I laughed. "What did they say to that?"

"Though it struck me as odd, Carla—not Roberto—took the lead in answering the question about his friends. She assured me that the shooting was an accident and that neither man constituted a threat toward you."

"Was Carla even there Friday night?" I mused. "I mean, I didn't meet her at the party."

"No, I'm pretty certain she *wasn't* there because she said that based on what Roberto told her, everyone was drunk, angry, and resurrecting old grudges," Mom said. "Roberto backed up Carla's assertions, but he didn't volunteer any new information."

"He didn't when they were here yesterday

either." I sighed. "I'd love to be able to talk with Roberto alone and try to get his version of events unfiltered by Carla."

"Maybe you can. Before I asked about Blake and Todd and expressed my fear over you living in that gangster-infested town, we talked about some of the things they'd need in order to do the Depression-era setup right," she said. "I told them everything I could think of off the top of my head but said I'd probably come up with more throughout the day. You know how set and costume ideas often come to me while I'm thinking about or doing other things."

"Do I ever," I said.

"Anyway, Carla mentioned that if I thought of anything else, she'd be out of the office the rest of the day today but that Roberto would be in until around six o'clock."

"Thanks, Mom. I'll call right now."

"Keep me posted," she said before hanging up.

I went into my office and got the business card Roberto had given me before he and Carla had left yesterday. I dialed the number and a man answered on the second ring. I thought it was Roberto, but I wasn't entirely sure.

"Hi, this is Marcy Singer calling. Is Roberto or Carla there?"

"This is Roberto. Carla and I spoke with your mom this morning. She's an incredible lady."

"She is," I agreed. "She was thrilled that you and Carla were so knowledgeable and appreciative of her work."

"Thanks for putting us in touch with her," said Roberto. "I've already talked with the guy she referred us to for the Depression-era movie, and Carla and I have an appointment to see him tomorrow. We believe he's going to be a perfect fit for this project."

"I'm glad Mom and I could help." I felt my conscience pinch me when I asked, "Is Carla there?"

"No, she's out. Is there something I could help you with?"

"Well, as you know, I've been wanting to talk with Tawny Milligan about the guys and their past histories, stuff like that," I said. "Since Carla said she and Tawny had been friends at one point, I thought maybe she could fill me in on—"

"There's no point," Roberto interrupted. "Tawny is gone. Forget about her. She couldn't contribute anything to the defense or to the prosecution either, for that matter, because no one has seen her in over ten years. If you want to know what happened Friday night, I'll tell you. Graham pushed Blake to the breaking point, and Blake shot him."

"Are you sure?" I asked quietly.

"Positive. I saw Blake get Todd's gun out of his office. But please don't repeat that," he said, his voice losing the excitement it held mere seconds ago and becoming so quiet I could barely hear him. "Carla doesn't want us to get embroiled in a trial that could put us months behind our production schedule. That would cost us a fortune. So . . . not a word. Please. Not even to Carla, okay?"

"Sure," I said.

"Look, I gotta run. Take care, Marcy."

I managed to mumble "You too" before ending the call. I dropped my phone onto the ottoman and ran into the bathroom. I felt nauseous, so I wet a washcloth with cold water and bathed my face. I began sobbing and sank onto the cool tile floor.

Roberto's scenario made no sense. None of it made any sense. Why would Blake shoot Graham? Over Graham wanting Blake to open MacKenzies' Mochas franchises? That would be stupid. No matter how drunk Blake might've been—and he hadn't seemed all that drunk when Sadie and I saw him at the jail—he wouldn't have shot Graham over something as inconsequential as that.

Maybe Roberto was mistaken. He said he saw Blake take Todd's gun from his office, but maybe it was something else . . . something Roberto had *thought* was a gun. Or maybe Graham had been threatening someone, and Blake took the gun intending to scare Graham off or something. Or Blake might've shot Graham in self-defense . . . although that didn't make sense when there was only one gun found in the room.

No, no, no! Roberto was wrong. Blake couldn't have shot Graham Stott. He couldn't have.

A furry face pressed against mine. I lowered the washcloth and hugged Angus. He began licking my face and right ear.

Suddenly, Todd appeared in the bathroom doorway. I'd been crying so hard, I hadn't heard the bells jingle when the front door had opened.

He stooped down and hauled me gently to my feet. "Marcy, are you okay?"

Fresh tears spilled onto my cheeks, and he pulled me into his arms.

"What's wrong?" he asked. "What's happened?"

I jerked away from him and buried my face in the washcloth. *He* should've told me what happened Friday night. He shouldn't have let me get blindsided by Roberto Gutierrez.

Whether Roberto's story was accurate or not, his version should not have been the first one I heard.

I had to hand it to Todd, though. He wasn't about to be put off that easily. Placing his hands on my shoulders, he said, "I'm here for you. Please don't push me away. I want to help you through whatever it is that has you so upset."

I flung the washcloth into the sink and turned to glare up at him. "If you'd been honest with me, I wouldn't *be* this upset right now!"

"Is it Keira? You still won't believe I'm not involved with her? Look, I know I shouldn't have dragged my feet on asking you to the masquerade ball last month. And then I shouldn't have got jealous because you were going with Ted and asked Keira to go with me. But I did. Now I regret all that, but—"

"This is not about you, Keira, or the stupid masquerade ball!"

"I know," Todd said. "It's about the hand-holding yesterday."

I let out a screech of frustration. "This is not about you at all! Roberto Gutierrez just told me that Blake shot Graham with your gun! Now, you either tell me right now exactly what happened on Friday night, or you get out of my shop . . . and don't ever come back!"

"All right. Okay, I'll tell you," he said. "Can we go into your office or something so we can sit down?"

"Yes. Go on into the office, and I'll be right there." I went to the front door, locked it, and put the clock on the door that said I'd be back in half an hour. It was roughly lunchtime, so people would think I'd simply gone out for something to eat.

When I stepped into the office, Todd was sitting on the straight-back chair beside my desk. He looked pale. I sat down on the desk chair, stared at Todd, and waited.

"I'm not sure exactly what happened . . . even though Blake and I have been over it at least a dozen times since yesterday," he said huskily. "It was all over in a heartbeat. I heard the gunshot, I hit the ground, not knowing what was going on, and then I rolled over and saw Blake standing there with the gun."

"Start at the beginning," I said, my voice softer and no longer accusatory.

"Okay. You were there shortly after the beginning," he said. "You saw that everybody was in a decent mood, laughing and joking around. And you saw that we were drinking pretty steadily."

"I did notice that."

"We were there to have a good time." He swiped his hands over his face. "I didn't consider that not everybody has fun when they get loose. Some people make trouble."

"Like Graham."

He nodded. "Like Graham. Actually, I think he'd already been drinking before he got to the Brew Crew because it didn't take much alcohol to put him in an ornery mood. And then he started trying to pick a fight."

"With Blake?" I asked.

"With everyone. He called the Brew Crew a dirty little dive. He threw out a dig at Andy about his teaching job and then one at Mark for not being intelligent enough to do anything other than build up his muscles for a living. He called Roberto an Oliver Stone wannabe, and he said Charles was a hack."

"What about Blake? Someone told me Graham was trying to get him to offer franchises of MacKenzies' Mochas," I said.

"Yeah, but that's not what made Blake angry," said Todd. "Graham and Sadie dated before she got together with Blake."

"I heard that too."

"Well, Graham never quite got over the fact that Sadie dumped him for Blake," he said. "So it wasn't so much that Graham wanted a coffeehouse franchise. He wanted to be close to Sadie. He'd have loved another chance with her. Heck, he'd have liked to have had her in his life by any means possible, and he didn't make much of a secret about it."

"But she and Blake are married," I said. "Graham couldn't just wish that away."

"Well, that's where he stepped across the line." Todd stood. "Can I get a bottle of water from your fridge?"

"Sure. Help yourself."

He got the water, opened it, and took a long drink before sitting back down. "Graham threatened Blake's marriage."

"How could he do that?" I asked. "Blake and Sadie have been married for five years— *happily* married. Graham couldn't break up their marriage on a whim."

"Yeah, well . . ." He lowered his eyes to the floor.

"You don't think Sadie still had any interest in Graham, do you?" I asked.

"No. But I don't think she knew about Blake and Tawny Milligan," he said.

"They dated? So what?" I couldn't see how that was a big deal all these years after the fact.

"So when Tawny left college, there were rumors that she was pregnant."

I started shaking my head. "Blake was with Sadie then. He wouldn't have fathered a child with another woman."

"No, he wouldn't have," said Todd. "He *didn't*. At least, I don't think he did. But Graham knew Blake had never told Sadie about Tawny. And all he'd have to do is plant that doubt."

"Where's Tawny now?" I asked. "Robbie mentioned her to me on Saturday, and I've been trying to find her ever since. It's like she disappeared off the face of the earth."

"It would be just as well if she did," he said softly. "If you want to help Blake at all, don't bring that woman here."

I clasped my hands together tightly. "Are you telling me you think Blake could be the father of Tawny's baby?" When Todd was silent, I continued. "Or are you saying Blake really did shoot Graham Stott?"

"Graham and I were in the back room, and I was trying to convince him to leave. I was calling a cab for him." Todd took another drink from his water bottle. "He was arguing with me. I heard the shot, and the rest happened like I told you. When I talked with Blake, he told me he didn't shoot Graham. But if he didn't, who did?"

Chapter Thirteen

After Todd left, I went into the bathroom to wash my face and to reapply my makeup. Todd was going to talk with Blake and Sadie later today to see if we could all meet at my house this evening after my class. Since it was such a gorgeous afternoon, he'd taken Angus to play at the beach first. I think mainly Todd wanted to clear his head and enjoy the freedom of romping on the beach. Freedom had to feel divine after spending the weekend locked up in jail. And, of course, Todd was faced with the knowledge that if he was convicted, he might lose his freedom for a lot longer than a weekend.

Who could blame him for holding hands with Keira? Or with anyone else, for that matter? He and I had hardly dipped our toes into the dating pond, and I'd also been out with Ted. Maybe Todd was simply being as cautious as I was.

I unlocked the front door and then settled into my favorite chair with the Mountmellick embroidery project. I hadn't had as much time to work on it as I would have liked. Still, it was coming along nicely, albeit slowly. Somewhere in the midst of my daisy-petal stitching, Andy called. He said he wanted to apologize for being rude during dinner Sunday evening.

"There you were, kind enough to buy me a meal, and I behaved like a jerk," he said.

"Oh, no, you didn't," I said. "I'm the one who was asking inappropriate questions."

"You were only trying to help your friends, Marcy. It's just that I'm touchy whenever the subject of Tawny Milligan comes up."

"It appeared to me that she'd been more to you than merely the cleaning lady . . . at least, at some point."

"I loved her," he said simply. "She was the first girl I ever fell for. But it was embarrassing to me because . . . well, I don't think she felt the same way. Anyway, the reason I'm calling is to ask you to let me make it up to you."

"There's no need to do that," I said.

"Please," he said. "I'd like to. May I take you out tomorrow night?"

"I'm sorry, but I can't. I have embroidery classes on Tuesday, Wednesday, and Thursday evenings."

"Oh. Yeah. Okay . . . maybe some other time, then."

I could hear the dejection in his voice and quickly said, "I'm free on Friday."

"Really? That's super," he said. "We can have dinner on Friday night, then?"

"That would be nice." Sure it would. Like I needed any more drama in my life. But he'd sounded so sad . . . and I *had* deceived him initially . . . and I *had* struck a nerve with him about Tawny Milligan and brought up hurt feelings. Besides, he may be able to give me more information on what happened at the Brew Crew on the night of the murder as long as I avoided bringing up Tawny ever again.

Shortly after I'd talked with Andy, a couple of women came into the shop to browse. I greeted them, told them to let me know if they needed help with anything, and then allowed them to look around as they pleased.

One noticed the Mountmellick piece I was working on. She was a tall, pencil-thin redhead with dark green eyes.

"That's lovely," she said. "Brenda, come look at this!"

Brenda, a brunette with her hair in a messy updo, hurried over from the other side of the shop to see what her friend had discovered. "Ooh! That *is* pretty. Is it hard to do?"

"Not really. This is my first Mountmellick project," I said. "I got the books in because I wanted to have some Irish embroidery patterns on hand in honor of Saint Patrick's Day. When I began looking through one of the books, I fell in love with the style and had to try it myself."

"Wow. That's cool," the redhead said. "Where are the books?"

I stood and led them over to the rack holding the Mountmellick books. They sat down in the sit-and-stitch square and within minutes were ready to buy the materials needed to make their own pieces. Luckily, I'd had the foresight to stock several yards of white denim, and varying weights of white floss for the various Mountmellick stitches.

As the women checked out, I asked if they'd be interested in taking embroidery classes.

"I might be," Brenda said.

I placed a flyer in her bag and asked her to call me if she had any questions.

They were leaving the Seven-Year Stitch as Mark, the personal trainer, was coming in. I noticed them both giving him admiring glances. He didn't seem to pay attention to them other than to politely hold the door open for them to pass through. The women thanked him, stepped out onto the sidewalk, and then turned to look at Mark again. They were whispering and giggling as they walked away.

"I believe you made their day," I said.

"Now they know chivalry isn't dead, I guess." He smiled. "Do you have your weights?"

"I do. They're in my office, if you'd like to come on back."

"You have a nice place here," Mark said, looking around the shop appreciatively as he followed me to the office. "I like how you've set the seating area apart. It's almost as if it's another room, and yet it's inclusive."

"Thank you. You have a keen eye for detail. I liked how you had your gym set up too." I laughed. "I'd have hated to have had to work on my exercises in front of guys who so obviously knew what they were doing when I just as obviously didn't."

"Yeah, well, when people pay for private instruction, it should be private," he said.

"I agree wholeheartedly." I remembered

Todd telling me that Graham had criticized Mark for making his living off his muscles rather than his brain. "People who don't own their own businesses have no idea how hard it can be."

"Ain't that the truth?"

We reached my office, and Mark spotted my dumbbells on the floor by my desk. He grinned. "I didn't realize someone had designed a line of fairy-tale princess sporting goods."

"Oh, sure. They had pink ones, too, but I thought those were a tad over the top."

"Unlike these," he said, picking both up in one large hand and holding them out toward me. "Let's see what you've got."

I began doing the biceps curls.

Mark straightened my wrists. "Like this. . . . There you go."

The shop's doorbells jingled.

"Would you please excuse me for just one second?" I handed Mark the dumbbells. I stepped into the shop and saw that it was Todd and Angus who'd come in.

"Come say hi to Mark," I said, mainly to let Todd know we weren't alone. I wouldn't want him to blurt out anything—especially about the case or Blake—that he wouldn't want Mark or anyone else to hear.

"Mark's here?" Todd asked with a frown.

I nodded. "He's checking out my form."

Angus had already bounded into the office to see who was there. When Todd and I walked into the room, Mark was rubbing the dog's tummy.

Mark and Todd shook hands.

"How's everything going, man?" Mark asked.

"It's going." Todd gave a weak smile. "I'm trying to have faith that everything will be all right."

"If there's anything I can do, let me know," Mark said. He handed me the dumbbells. "Marcy, let's see your overhead triceps extensions."

"Sorry for interrupting," Todd said. "You guys get back to work, and I'll talk with you later, Marce. Thanks for letting me borrow Angus."

"Anytime," I said.

Angus followed Todd back into the shop—probably thinking they were going to return to the beach—as I demonstrated my triceps extensions to Mark. I had very good form on that one, by the way.

I tried to engage Mark in conversation about entrepreneurship, self-employment critics, Todd . . .

Nothing. The guy was singularly focused on the task at hand. After checking—and often adjusting—my form on each of the exercises he'd given me to do, he told me he'd check back on me in a couple of weeks to see how I was progressing. And then he left. Mark was the epitome of the "strong, silent type."

By the time Mark left, it was around three o'clock. Since I usually had a slump about that time—I guessed it was due to school being dismissed around then—I took a bottle of water and my phone to the sit-and-stitch square and called Riley.

"Hi," I said quietly when she answered the phone. "Is this a bad time?"

"No. Why are you whispering?" she asked. "Is anything wrong?"

"No. And now I feel utterly stupid. I was whispering because I thought the baby might be sleeping."

We both laughed.

"Actually, she *is* sleeping," Riley said. "But how are *you* doing? Suddenly, it's you I'm worried about."

"I'm all right . . . just a little loopy. How are you holding up?"

"I'm doing great. Laura is only waking up about once during the night," she said. "I'm hoping she'll start sleeping all the way through by the time I have to head back to work in a couple weeks. Mom says I'm being overly optimistic, but I think Laura and I will have worked out an agreeable schedule by then."

"I hope so," I said. "How's Keith?"

"He still has his head in the clouds," she said with a giggle in her voice. "However, he does come back to earth for diaper duty, feedings, and snuggle time—with Laura and with me."

"That's sweet."

"Yeah . . . So tell me what's going on with the murder investigation," she said.

"I imagine you've heard about the arraignment," I said.

"I have. I'm a little surprised at Judge Street granting bail. Cam must've been fairly convincing on the 'strong community ties' argument."

"He was," I said. "And Blake's attorney pretty much said 'Ditto.' "

Riley groaned. "I don't know why in the world Blake went with McQuiston. He's competent in other areas, but he has almost no criminal law experience."

"I believe he's a friend of Sadie's parents," I told her.

"Well, there are friends of the family, and

then there's somebody like Cam Whitting who can keep your butt out of prison for life." She expelled a long breath. "Sorry. I shouldn't have said that. But that sort of thing really strikes a nerve with me. I've seen so many—" She stopped herself from finishing the thought. "So, what else is new?"

"Not a lot," I said. "I've been doing what I can to help, which isn't much. I'd hoped to talk with some of the fraternity brothers and their friends to see if anyone had any long-standing grudges with Graham."

"And what did you dig up?"

"Well, one name that keeps popping up is that of Tawny Milligan. I tried to get in touch with her, but I can't find her. Were you and Todd dating while he was in college?" I asked. "I thought that, if so, you might've known Tawny, since she was friends with so many of the Alpha Sigs."

"Todd and I were together his last year at OSU, so, yeah, I did know Tawny. She was standoffish toward me, and I chalked that up to her being jealous because she was a little infatuated with Todd."

"Had she and Todd dated before?"

"No. Blake had dated Tawny briefly," Riley said. "Even if Todd had been interested in

Tawny, he'd have adhered to the unwritten guy rule that says you don't date the girl who dumped your best friend."

"Are you telling me Sadie was Blake's rebound?" I asked incredulously.

"Well, she was obviously more than that. I mean, look how long the two of them have been together. Right?"

"Yeah." I tried to dispel the doubt nagging in my noggin. "Who else did Tawny date?"

"She ultimately wound up with Graham—who broke her heart, by the way, and might be why she left OSU, never to be heard from again," she said. "But in addition to her dating Graham, it was rumored that she'd also had flings—or more like one-night stands—with Roberto and Andy."

"How about Mark or Charles?" I asked. "Did she have any sort of relationship with them?"

"She was friends with both of them. That was the extent of it, as far as I know."

"She must have been very beautiful," I said. "Roberto's wife said she had violet eyes like Elizabeth Taylor's."

Riley laughed softly. "Carla would've clawed those violet eyes out of Tawny's head if she'd known about Tawny and Roberto. But, yeah, Tawny was pretty enough. Not Elizabeth Taylor stunning but certainly not ugly."

"I'm just dying to see what this seductress looks like. Don't forget, Sadie and I didn't go to OSU. And Sadie never even met Tawny."

"That's not surprising," she said. "I can't imagine Tawny would want to meet the woman that Graham was so enamored of."

"Sadie's relationship with Graham confuses me too. She and I were roommates in college, but I'd never met Graham until Friday night at the party," I said. "I did notice that Sadie wasn't with Blake and the group of fraternity guys when I went by to pick her up, but I supposed she just didn't want to hang out with a group of guys. Sadie didn't mention that she and Graham had dated."

"She and Graham only went out for a couple of months. Sadie was a freshman then. . . ."

"That explains it. Sadie was at the school for a year and had already changed majors by the time I got there. I am surprised, though, that Sadie never mentioned their relationship," I said. "Especially after Friday."

"Maybe she was just too caught up in worrying about Blake's predicament . . . and her own, for that matter. I mean, if Blake goes to prison, what will that mean for her and for the coffeehouse?" asked Riley. "Besides, I don't think her relationship with Graham was all that serious as far as Sadie was concerned. Like I told you, Graham was head over heels for her. But after he introduced Sadie to Blake, those two only had eyes for each other. I'm not sure Graham ever forgave Blake for that."

"What was to forgive?" I asked. "They couldn't help the way they felt about each other."

"True. But you have to admit, if you introduced the guy you loved to one of your best friends, and they hooked up, you'd be pretty ticked at both of them," she said. "And Graham was definitely ticked. He'd still try to act like he was Blake's buddy, but he'd undermine him every chance he got."

I could hear Laura beginning to fuss in the background. "It sounds like duty calls."

"More like *doody* calls," Riley said with a bark of laughter.

"Give her a kiss for me . . . you know . . . after the cleanup. I'll be by to see you guys soon."

Chapter Fourteen

Sadie came into the Seven-Year Stitch just as I was getting ready to lock up and take Angus home. I always took him home, fed him, and let him out into the backyard before returning for class.

Sadie was carrying a MacKenzies' Mochas takeout bag. "I brought that chicken salad croissant I promised you yesterday. In fact, I've got us both one. Would you mind if I went with you to take Angus home?"

"Not at all," I said. "I'm happy for the company—the *extra* company, I mean." I patted Angus on the head.

I put my clock sign on the door indicating I'd be back by six p.m. for class. Then I locked the door, and Sadie, Angus, and I went out to the Jeep. I opened the back door on the driver's side, and Angus hopped in. I put up the pet barrier to keep him out of the front seat, but he could still hang his head over the front to be petted by Sadie during the drive home.

I wondered what Sadie wanted to talk with me about that she didn't want to discuss in front of Blake and Todd. Since Sadie hadn't told me Blake's version of Friday night's events, I didn't have a clue what she believed happened. Furthermore, I didn't know what Sadie knew—or maybe more importantly what she *didn't* know, since she'd never met Tawny Milligan—about Blake's time in college before she began dating him. I decided my best bet was to keep my mouth shut until Sadie opened up with whatever was on her mind.

She didn't say much until after we arrived at my house. While I fed Angus, Sadie got out plates and placed our croissants on them. She added the sea salt chips and brownies she'd also brought with her. I got us a couple of diet sodas—to offset the brownie calories, of course—and we sat down at the table. Angus abandoned his bowl to see if he could score bites of our dinner. With those big brown eyes? Of course he could.

Finally, Sadie started talking. "Todd told

Blake and me that you felt betrayed . . . that you thought we didn't trust you enough to tell you what happened on Friday night."

I didn't really have a response to that, so I had a bite of my croissant.

"We trust you," she continued. "We're just not sure of what happened ourselves. Even after Blake and Todd had their little private sit-down, Blake walked out not knowing any more than he had going in. What did Todd tell you?"

I took a drink of my soda. Then I looked Sadie in the eye. And . . . I took another drink. I realized there was no courage in the bottom of a soda glass. So I took a deep breath and told her, "Todd thinks Blake shot Graham. If he did, I know it had to be self-defense."

Sadie shook her head. "Blake did *not* shoot Graham. Graham was arguing with Todd, and he kept getting more and more aggressive. Blake overheard Graham threaten to kill Todd, so he got Todd's gun from his office and rushed to the back room where Todd and Graham were arguing." She took a steadying breath. "As Blake got to the doorway, he heard a shot ring out. At first, he thought Graham had shot Todd because Todd immediately hit the floor facedown. But then he saw that Graham had also fallen, only Graham had fallen onto his back and Blake could see that he was bleeding. Blake dropped the gun onto the floor and went to check on the men."

"Where was the gun that was used to kill Graham?" I asked.

"I don't know. Blake said he didn't see it," said Sadie. "And as nice as it is that Todd's playing the hero like he's protecting Blake, he's got it backward. Blake has been protecting Todd. *He's* the one who shot Graham."

"Would you and Blake come over after class so you can talk with Todd and me?" I asked. "Maybe the four of us together can figure out what actually happened and why."

"Sure. I'm fine with that. If nothing else, it'll get me out from under Mom's thumb for a while."

I bit my lip. "They're still staying with you?"

"I'm afraid so."

"Once again, I'm sorry about that," I said.

"You meant well." Her words were forgiving, but her tone was not.

Class was . . . interesting. Reggie was there. Julie and her teenage daughter, Amber, were there—they were two of my most loyal students and had been taking classes since I first opened the Seven-Year Stitch. Vera was in at-

tendance, and surprisingly enough, so was
Margaret Trelawney. Since her husband Bill
died, Mrs. Trelawney had been my landlord.
She sometimes dropped in on my classes, but
she had never signed up for one, nor had she
ever worked on an embroidery project.

As the students came in, I offered them a
bottle of water. I also took their coats and jack-
ets and hung them on the rack in my office.
When I returned to the sit-and-stitch area, Mrs.
Trelawney was unwrapping a Starlight mint
she'd taken from the bowl I'd put in the center
of the coffee table.

I sat down beside Mrs. Trelawney on the
sofa. "I'm so glad you could make it this evening," I said. "How's Sylvia?" Her sister-in-
law had acted like a shrew when Mr. Trelawney
had first died, but she appeared to have mel-
lowed within the past few months.

"She's fine," Mrs. Trelawney said. "She's
driving down this coming weekend, and I'm
going to go back home to Portland with her for
a few days. We're going to do some shopping."

"That'll be fun," I said.

"It will be unless she starts making an issue
of how much of Bill's hard-earned money I'm
spending." Mrs. Trelawney huffed. "But I'll
have her know he didn't earn it all by himself.

And another thing: he's gone now, so that money belongs to me."

I turned to the group in general. "How did everyone do on her project this week?"

They—with the singular exception of Mrs. Trelawney—began taking their works in progress out of their tote bags. Everyone's project was progressing nicely, and since no one had any immediate questions, we got to work. As we stitched, we talked about Manu's homecoming and Riley's beautiful baby girl. Inevitably, the subject of Graham Stott's murder arose.

"That was a terrible ordeal at the Saint Patrick's Day party," Julie said softly, brushing the light brown hair out of her eyes. "Have the police figured out what happened?"

"I don't think all the facts in the case are known yet," I said.

"Who had a party, and what happened?" Mrs. Trelawney asked. "I miss all the fun."

Reggie broke the group's collective awkward silence by saying, "The party was at the Brew Crew, and Graham Stott was shot."

"Who'd he shoot?" Mrs. Trelawney demanded. "That Graham always was an impudent cuss. I'm not a bit surprised he had the gall to shoot somebody."

"No, dear," Vera said gently. "Graham was

the victim. He's the person who got shot. I get what you're saying, though. Graham always reminded me of an Eddie Haskell type—always buttering people up so he could try and get away with something."

"Somebody shot Eddie Haskell?" Mrs. Trelawney unwrapped another mint and popped it into her mouth.

If I thought I could have gotten away with rolling my eyes, I would have.

"It was probably Ward or Wally," Mrs. Trelawney said. "Did Eddie do something mean to the Beav?"

"More than likely," Reggie said.

"No, wait. I remember now." Mrs. Trelawney raised her index finger to her lips. "Eddie was shot in the line of duty after he became a police officer. He was saved by his bullet-proof vest and his belt buckle."

"Wow," I said. "That's something."

Reggie deftly changed the subject back to stitching with a question about the piece she was working on. I was truly grateful. Sometimes, Mrs. Trelawney seemed sword-tip sharp. But at other times, she made me wonder what kind of medications she was taking. And she did tend to go off on the strangest tangents. For example, after class, she took me aside.

"While I simply adore your little soirees, you need to consider serving more satisfying refreshments," she said. I'd heard this one before. She kindly pointed out to me almost every time she came that my snacks were somewhat lacking.

"Actually, Mrs. Trelawney, these are embroidery classes," I replied.

"Perhaps I can bring something the next time. I do so wish that Tawny Milligan still ran her mother's catering business. I thought of her because she used to date that cheeky Graham Stott, you know."

I placed my hand on Mrs. Trelawney's forearm. "You know Tawny Milligan?"

"Oh, yes. She makes the best tarts," said Mrs. Trelawney. "I mentioned that to Graham once—I thought they were going to get married and that he'd be proud to have a wife who was such an accomplished baker."

"And was he proud?" I asked.

"No. He said it took a great tart to make one, he guessed." She narrowed her eyes and shook her head. "He was repugnant."

"It sounds like it. Where's Tawny now?"

"I don't know," she said. "She left town. One could hardly blame her for that."

"Because of Graham?"

Mrs. Trelawney nodded. "And the pregnancy, of course."

I gaped. "Tawny Milligan was pregnant?" Then Todd's guess had been spot-on. "Was the child Graham's?"

"I suppose. She left, and I never heard any more about it." She brightened. "Have a good night, Marcy, darling. And do think about what I said."

I nodded. I'd be thinking about what she said, all right, but it would be about Tawny Milligan's baby rather than soiree refreshments. After that revelation, it didn't bother me overmuch that Mrs. Trelawney thought I'd hosted a party and had served water and Starlight mints.

Reggie had hung back until after the other students and Mrs. Trelawney left. "I heard back from my friend Carol. The name Tawny Milligan used after she left college was Sarah Masterson," said Reggie. "The number Carol had for her had been disconnected, though, and my own Internet search didn't produce any solid leads."

"Did Carol mention anything about Tawny being pregnant?" I asked.

"No. Was she?"

"According to Mrs. Trelawney, she was. Of course, Mrs. Trelawney thinks I threw a party this evening and served only Starlight mints. And water." Okay, so it bothered me a little.

Reggie burst out laughing. "She can get terribly confused. What else did she say about Tawny?"

"She said Tawny used to run her mother's catering business and was an excellent baker."

"That much is true," Reggie said. "I remember that catering company. It was located in Lincoln City and was called A Special Occasion. I'll look it up and see if it's still there."

"Cool. Please let me know what you find out," I said.

"I will. I'm pretty curious about this name change and mysterious disappearance myself."

When I got home, Sadie, Blake, and Todd were already waiting for me. Since Sadie had a key, they'd let Angus in and had made a pot of decaffeinated coffee. The three of them were sitting around the table sipping coffee and looking glum when I walked into the kitchen. Even Angus looked sad, but he stood and greeted me.

I hugged him and kissed the top of his scruffy head. "Everything is okay, baby." I looked at Sadie. "Everything *is* all right, isn't it?"

THE LONG STITCH GOOD NIGHT 213

"I guess so," she said. "All things considered."

I, too, sat down at the table. I noticed that everyone else was having trouble making eye contact. We'd never get anywhere like this. Someone needed to take the plunge. I figuratively held my nose and dived in.

"So, guys, each of you believes the other one shot Graham Stott," I said. "I realize you've been over this ad nauseam in your own heads and among yourselves, and I understand you're best friends and you're trying to protect each other. But it might help if you lay the facts out individually so Sadie and I can get a fresh take on what happened Friday night. So, one at a time—starting with Blake, which makes it alphabetical—tell me what took place at the Brew Crew party. And start at the beginning of the evening."

Blake breathed deeply, stared down at the table, and started talking. "When Sadie and I first got to the Brew Crew, everything was cool. Everybody—the Alpha Sigs, I mean— seemed to be relaxed and having a good time. Sadie saw someone she knew, and she went over to say hello."

"Were all the Alpha Sigs there then?" I asked.

"Not at that time. Mark and Graham hadn't got there yet," Blake said. "While Sadie was talking with her friend, Graham came in. Sadie and Graham had a history, and Sadie doesn't—didn't—like him, so she stayed at the bar after that."

"Is that when the mood started turning sour?" I got up to get a cup of coffee and to top off everyone else's.

"Not right away," Blake answered. "I mean, Graham was a little snooty as usual, and he appeared to be already a little buzzed when he got there. But he didn't get belligerent until after he'd had more to drink."

"From what I've heard, it didn't take long for the trouble to start." I returned the coffeepot to its base and sat back down.

"No, it didn't." Blake raked his hands through his short blond hair. "We all had too much to drink Friday night. We should've known better."

"Nope," I said. "We're not having a shoulda-coulda-woulda or a pity party here. Just tell us what happened as you remember it."

"Yeah, okay," said Blake. "Basically, as the night progressed, Graham got more and more argumentative with everyone. Finally, I heard him arguing with Todd. I don't know what they were fighting about, but Graham threatened to kill Todd. I distinctly heard Graham say the words *I'll kill you*. So I ran into Todd's office and got the gun. I was going to threaten Graham and make him leave. As I got to the back room, I heard the shot fire. Both Graham and Todd hit the floor. I dropped the gun and went to see if they were okay. And you know the rest."

"All right." I nodded toward Todd. "Your turn."

"Blake is spot-on up until the point where he ran into the back room. Graham and I *were* arguing," Todd said.

"Why did he threaten to kill you?" I asked.

"He was just blowing smoke. I took his keys away and told him I was calling a cab." He sipped his coffee. "He really was too drunk to go driving off, and I refused to give him back his keys. He said his car was a Bentley Continental GT and that he refused to leave it parked at this *dive* overnight. He said to give him his keys or he'd kill me. I wasn't in fear for my life. I knew he was just talking."

"And this is what you were arguing about in the back room?" Blake asked. "I thought it was . . . you know . . . something more serious."

"What did you think it was?" Sadie asked her husband.

Blake and Todd shared a look, and then Blake shook his head. "I don't know."

"Yes you do," Sadie said.

"And if we're going to sort this out and help you two, you have to be up front with us," I added.

"Like we've both said, Graham was arguing with everybody," Todd said. "He was bringing up all this junk from the past as well as the present. Sadie had mentioned to Charles that Riley went into labor. Since Riley and I had dated my last year of college, all the guys knew her. Charles suggested we drink a toast to her."

"Graham began taunting Todd," Blake said. "He asked how it felt to know the woman he loved was giving birth to another man's child."

"I made it clear to Graham that I wasn't in love with Riley," said Todd, directing his answer to me.

"But Graham wouldn't let up," said Blake. "He just kept hammering at Todd about how Riley had dumped him for Keith and that Keith had been the better man then and was still the better man."

"And then, of course, I had to remind him that Sadie had dumped him for Blake, who was by far a better man than Graham would ever be." Todd raised his coffee cup in a salute to Blake. "From there, things just went from bad to worse. I should've never brought up Sadie to Graham when he'd been drinking."

"Not that he was that crazy about me," Sadie said. "He just never liked to lose anything. While we were dating, he looked at me as being *his*, and we didn't even go out for all that long. He simply staked his claim, and I was supposed to adhere to it until he was finished with me." She reached over and took Blake's hand. "But I met this guy, and fell in love almost immediately."

"Ditto." Blake leaned in for a kiss.

"You guys previously said that Graham was being a jerk to everybody," I said. "Was that before or after the Riley toast?"

"Both," Todd said. "He started with Mark. When Mark arrived, Graham asked him where he'd been. Mark said he had to finish up at the gym before he could leave, and Graham said it's too bad he had more brawn than brain and couldn't manage a white-collar job."

"Let me guess," I said. "Mark just blew him off."

"How'd you know?" Blake asked.

"Because in the short time I've known Mark, he seems unfazed by just about everything," I said.

"Don't let him fool you," said Todd. "If he's pushed too far, he will retaliate."

"Did Graham pick on any of the other guys?" Sadie asked.

"Sure, but it was just petty stuff," Blake said. "Nothing happened that you'd expect Graham to be murdered over."

"Nothing happened *there*," I said. "Or nothing happened on Friday night that you guys know of. But something obviously happened that put Graham on someone's hit list. We just have to figure out what and whose list."

"I say we add *how* to that list." Blake shook his head. "There were three people in that room: Graham, Todd, and me. Unless Graham shot himself, I don't know how it could've happened without Todd or me seeing who did it."

"I think the shooter was in the hallway behind you," I said to Blake. "After he shot Graham, he could've run into the bathroom or blended into the crowd."

"That would explain why there wasn't another gun found," Todd said. "He took it with him."

Chapter Fifteen

The next morning, as soon as Angus and I got to the shop, I went into the office and logged on to the computer. A man as rich, powerful, and arrogant as Graham Stott was bound to have a few enemies. I wanted to try to find out who they were and if they could've been at the Brew Crew Friday night. A jury needed nothing more than reasonable doubt to return a not-guilty verdict. And although I was certain their attorneys—well, Todd's, anyway—were all over that, I wanted to help my friends in any way I could.

Before leaving my house last night, Blake and Todd had resolved to consult with their attorneys and, if the attorneys agreed, to tell their story to the police. Right now I feared law enforcement was working to build the prosecution's case against Blake and Todd rather than seeking other viable suspects. After all, they believed the killer or killers—Blake and Todd could theoretically have been working together—had already been indicted.

I stared at my empty search bar, wondering what to type. I supposed I could simply start with the name *Graham Stott*. But what I wanted to know is who would have profited from Graham's death. Had Todd and Blake not been found in the room with the victim and the possible murder weapon, the police would have started questioning the people who had the most to gain from killing the victim. So I keyed in *Graham Stott, Oregon, business partners*, and I clicked the search key. The screen instantly filled with links.

Before I could begin scrolling through them, the bells over the shop door jingled. I minimized the window and hurried out into the shop. My visitor was Andy, and he was playing ball with Angus.

"This is a great dog," Andy said. "Is he yours?"

"Yep. His name is Angus."

At the mention of his name, Angus came and dropped his ball at my feet. I picked it up and tossed it into the sit-and-stitch area.

As Angus scampered after his ball, I asked Andy if he had any pets.

"Not me," he said. "My landlord forbids it. My nephew has a Jack Russell terrier, though." He laughed. "And, believe me, those two rambunctious boys can get into a lot of trouble."

"I bet so."

Angus brought his ball back to Andy, and Andy dutifully lobbed it across the room.

"Would you like to sit down?" I asked.

"No, thanks," Andy said. "I can't stay but a minute. I don't have a class this morning until eleven, so I thought I'd come by and check out your shop on my way to school." He looked around and nodded approvingly. "This is super."

"Thank you so much." I grinned. "Let me give you the grand tour." I gestured to the right. "That's the shop area." I gestured to the left. "And this is the sit-and-stitch square."

"You didn't introduce me to your lovely assistant," he said with a smile.

"That's Jill. I'd planned to name her after Marilyn Monroe's character in *The Seven Year Itch*, but—"

"But Marilyn's character didn't have a name in that movie. They called her *the girl*," Andy finished.

"I'm impressed," I said. "Are you an old movie buff or a Marilyn fan?"

"A little of both." Angus returned with the ball, and Andy threw it again. "You look kinda like her. That's why I could hardly believe you'd go out with me . . . you know, you looking like you and me looking like me."

I leveled my gaze. "Stop fishing for compliments, Andy. You're just trying to get me to confirm that you're an attractive guy."

"So we're still on for Friday?" he asked.

"Of course. I have to be up front with you, though. I've dated some since moving to Tallulah Falls, but I'm pretty cautious," I said. "I didn't leave my heart in San Francisco, but I did have it trampled on there."

"Hey, I've had my share of heartbreak too. Friendship is good, though, right?"

"The best." I smiled. "By the way, Blake said Graham was taunting Todd because Riley had given birth to her and Keith's baby. But I thought Todd and Riley were through at least three years ago. Why would Graham taunt Todd about that now?"

Andy shrugged. "Some people say you never get over your first love. Graham hadn't got over his, and he didn't think Todd had either."

"And Graham's first love was Sadie?" I asked.

"Inasmuch as Graham ever loved anyone other than himself. Plus, I think in a way, he wanted Todd to commiserate with him," Andy said. "The Todd-Riley-Keith situation played out much like the Graham-Sadie-Blake scenario. When Riley met Keith, she broke things off with Todd to pursue the relationship with Keith."

"Graham sure had a perverse way of trying to garner sympathy," I said.

"Graham had a perverse way of doing a lot of things." He petted Angus. "I'd better get to the college. Should I pick you up here on Friday?"

"That should work. Give me a call Friday morning, and we'll work out the details," I suggested.

When Andy left, I went back into the office and pulled up the search engine results. As I perused the links, I wondered if it was possible that Todd *hadn't* gotten over his first love . . . if he still had feelings for Riley. Or maybe, like I'd seen with David—my ex-fiancé, who had tried his darnedest to get me back—time and distance had showed Todd that his and Riley's relationship wasn't the perfect pairing he'd once envisioned and that their romance wouldn't have lasted even had Keith not come into the picture.

My thoughts turned to Ted. His marriage hadn't lasted. He and his wife had—as far as I knew—gone through an amicable divorce. Ted never talked about it. In fact, I didn't even know his ex-wife's name. Did he avoid talking about her because he was still nursing a broken heart or because he was simply over her and had nothing to say?

It dawned on me that the two primary men pulling my heartstrings both had a ton of baggage. And it wasn't like I didn't have a matching set of my own that I was lugging around. But maybe Andy had the right idea with the friendship thing. It was possible that I was destined to play a "buddy girl" role to all the guys in this play rather than the girl the hero fell crazy in love with. Or it was possible that my hero had yet to arrive on the scene.

The doorbells jangled again, and I hopped up out of my office chair to return to the shop. Wouldn't it be wild if there was a handsome stranger standing there? Our eyes would meet, and the music would swell, and we would just *know*. There wouldn't be any waiting to see how things turned out. We'd know immediately that we were meant for each other.

The record scratched. . . .

Standing near the counter was not a handsome stranger but an attractive woman in her mid-forties with honey blond hair styled to perfection.

"Hello," I said. "Welcome to the Seven-Year Stitch."

"Thank you." She gave Angus a wary glance as he ambled up to her. "I'm guessing he's friendly, or else he wouldn't be here."

"He's very friendly," I told her. "But if it'll make you more comfortable, I can put him in another room while you shop."

"No, that's fine." She smiled warmly. "I do appreciate the offer, though. I've always been a little leery of dogs."

Angus, sensing his company was unwanted, went to stretch out at the window and people watch.

"Is there anything I can help you with?" I asked the customer.

"Maybe. I'm going to make bookmarks for my Bible study group. I'm debating between doing them in cross-stitch or Hardanger. Which do you think would be the better choice?"

I gave her question some thought. "While both are beautiful, I think cross-stitch bookmarks would be the better option because you can so easily customize your gifts to suit the group and the individuals."

The woman nodded. "Excellent point. Do you have any bookmark blanks?"

"Yes. Have you already got your pattern?"

"I do," she said. "All I'll need are the blanks, some flosses, and a roll of wide ribbon to sew onto the backs of the bookmarks to cover up my sloppy stitching."

I showed her where she could find everything she needed and handed her a small canvas shopping basket. "Please let me know if I can be of further help."

Ted came in as the woman was putting various colors of floss into her basket.

"Good morning," I told him.

"Hi." He turned his attention to Angus, who was happy a new playmate had arrived, especially since he'd been so recently rebuffed by the customer. "Want me to take him for a walk down the street?"

"That'd be great." I got Angus's leash and snapped it to his collar. "Thanks."

Ted smiled. "We'll be back in a few minutes."

By the time they returned, my customer had left.

"I really appreciate your taking Angus for a

walk," I said. Somewhere in the back of my mind, I could hear my mother's voice telling me to *allow him do something heroic whenever he's around*.

"No problem." He unfastened the leash and handed it back to me. "I figured it would do him good and give me something to do while that lady finished shopping. I wanted to talk with you privately."

"All right." I put the leash under the counter and followed Ted to the sofa facing away from the window. "Is anything wrong?"

"Calloway's attorney Cam Whitting called the head of the major crime team this morning demanding an explanation as to why his client was arrested and detained while Graham Stott's shooter is still at large," he said.

"But isn't that what attorneys are supposed to do?" I asked. "Profess their client's innocence?"

"Yeah, but what if the ballistics report comes in today and says that Calloway's gun wasn't the murder weapon? It'll look like I did a shoddy job." He leaned forward, placing his forearms on his knees. "My first big case filling in for Manu, and I'll have blown it."

"Ted, I know you. You're nothing if not thorough. No one could ever accuse you of botching an investigation."

"My team and I followed proper procedure," he said. "We interviewed every single person who was in the bar when we arrived. No one was allowed to leave until they'd spoken with us. We did an exhaustive search of the premises. . . . One of my guys even checked the toilet tanks to make sure no one had stashed a gun in one before we got there—you know, to hide it. We did everything by the book."

I placed a hand on his shoulder. "I'm sure you did. And there was no way you could've let Blake and Todd walk away when you discovered them in a room with a dead man and a gun . . . especially when they weren't willing to tell you what happened."

Ted leaned back against the sofa cushions and looked at me with surprise. "That means a lot, coming from you. I know how badly you want to believe they're innocent."

"I *do* believe they're innocent, but the fact that they're my friends doesn't negate that you did what you had to do," I said. "And I'm confident you'll find Graham Stott's killer and the evidence necessary to get a conviction."

"Did Calloway and MacKenzie tell you their story?" he asked.

I nodded. "Sadie, Blake, and Todd came to

my house last night and said each guy thought the other had shot Graham. That's why they didn't say anything initially."

"That's the story we got, too."

"You sound skeptical," I said.

"I am. They don't tell us this until they've been out of jail for two days? That seems a bit too convenient," said Ted. "But, of course, I'll keep looking at suspects and adding pieces to the puzzle until I get a clear picture." He took my hand. "What if the killer does turn out to be MacKenzie or Calloway?"

That was a question I wasn't prepared to answer.

That afternoon I was working on the Mountmellick project, Angus was lying near me gnawing on a chew toy, and a light rain had begun to fall. Growing up with a mother who was a Hollywood costume designer had made for a rich and creative fantasy life. And moments like these simply screamed for a daydream. My mind wandered into a film noir. The Seven-Year Stitch lost its color and became black-and-white. . . .

Of all the embroidery shops in all the little coastal towns in all the world, and he had to walk into mine. He wore a black trench coat, a dark gray fedora, and an air of danger. It was that danger that drew me to him . . . more so even than those compelling blue eyes or that devil-may-care mouth that said, "I'm Detective Ted Nash, and I've got a few questions for you."

I threw back my head. My hair was suddenly longer, curly, and falling seductively over my left eye. I couldn't see out of that one, but it was okay because the right eye was working good enough for the both of them. I pursed my very red lips. "You say you've got questions, gumshoe? Well, maybe I've got answers, and maybe I don't." I sashayed over to Ted, and somewhere in the distance a drummer beat out a soft boom-chica-boom-chica-boom. The drum stopped when I did.

"I think you do have answers," Ted told me. "Answers to things I don't even have questions for yet."

Suddenly, Todd burst through the door. As it was so eloquently stated in This Gun for Hire, he looked like he'd been on a hayride with Dracula. I said as much.

"Oh, yeah?" He rushed over and took me by the shoulders, spinning me away from Ted and toward him. His chocolate-colored eyes bored into my soul like sexy drill bits. "I've been framed, I tell ya. Framed like a Picasso and hung in the Louvre.

Framed by this guy." He jabbed a thumb toward Ted.

Ted broke in between us. "You don't know what you're talking about. I've got you dead to rights."

From somewhere— stage right, I supposed—an Elizabeth Taylor look-alike circa Cat on a Hot Tin Roof emerged. When she walked, she got the drum and a saxophone. She batted her violet eyes at the men, and I was pushed aside. I landed on the sofa like a heap of dirt and was just as forgotten.

"Tawny." Todd took her in his arms. "What are you doing here?"

"I grew a conscience, ya big lug," she drawled. "It wasn't this palooka that framed you. It was me." She stepped out of Todd's embrace and held her delicate wrists toward Ted. "Put the cuffs on me, copper, and haul me in."

"With pleasure." Ted said that lustily rather than with the satisfaction of a lawman doing his job.

"No," Todd protested. "She's lying. I did it. I killed Graham Stott, and I'd do it again for what he did to her."

"What'd he do to her?" I asked, but it was as if I wasn't even in this scene anymore.

"Good try," Ted said to Todd. Then to the woman he said, "I'm putting the bracelets on you, and you're coming with me, Toots." He clamped the handcuffs onto her wrists.

"Wait a second. What about me?" I asked.

Todd looked at me derisively. "What about *you*? You're not the kind of woman a fellow would go to prison for."

I dramatically whipped my face around to peer into Ted's eyes.

He shook his head almost sympathetically. "Sorry, kid. You're the kind of gal a man flirts with, but not the kind he marries. You don't set a guy's soul on fire."

Fade to black. . . .

I went back to stitching because, frankly, that fantasy scene sucked. It hadn't played it-self out in my mind quite the way I'd intended. Did I really think I was the kind of girl guys flirted with but didn't fall for? Apparently, I did. And I needed an attitude adjustment.

Chapter Sixteen

Thursday morning dawned as gray as my mood. I just hadn't been able to shake my melancholy attitude last night. Even the class could tell something was wrong. I told them I was just worried about the Graham Stott investigation and how it was affecting all my friends. That much was true, of course, but I'd have never admitted I was also feeling sorry for myself because Ted and Todd seemed to have lost interest in me.

I got out of bed determined that today Marcy Singer would be noticed . . . by someone. Andy had compared me to Marilyn Monroe. Well, today the comparison would be unmistakable. I put on a beige pencil skirt, a matching short-sleeved V-neck sweater, and black platform pumps. I curled my platinum hair, parted it on the right side, and let it fall just a bit over the left side of my face. Since my hair was short, it didn't cascade over my eye, and I was glad of that. That would get on my nerves in a hurry. I kept my makeup natural-looking, with the exceptions of bright red lipstick and heavy black eyeliner.

Now if only I had a drummer to tap out a *boom-chica-boom* when I walked. I giggled aloud at my own silliness, but it was amazing how much my mood had improved. I thought it was Marilyn Monroe who once said, "A wise girl kisses but doesn't love, listens but doesn't believe, and leaves before she is left." Maybe she was onto something.

Since it was pretty outside this morning, I left Angus playing in the backyard. When I went to start the Jeep, I was dismayed to learn that the battery was dead. Determined not to let it spoil my good mood, however, I decided to call a cab and to have the auto club bring me a new battery.

When the cab pulled up outside the Seven-Year Stitch, I opened the door, but the driver told me to wait. He got out and rushed around to help me out. I gave him his fare and a tip, and he asked if I needed for him to wait.

I laughed. "No, thank you. I can't afford to have you wait all day. I work here."

"My cab number is one-four-seven. Ask for me when you're ready to go back home," he said. "I'll be glad to drive you back."

"I'll keep that in mind." I got my key out of my purse and was unlocking the door when Captain Moe walked up.

"What are you doing, Tinkerbell? Trying to give an old man a triple bypass?" he asked, placing his hand on his chest.

"Never." My laughter bubbled over again. "Do you have time to come on in and visit with me?"

"It was what I was on my way to do. I've been to see Riley and the baby, and I wanted to stop by and say hello before heading for the diner."

I stepped into the shop and flipped on the lights. I stored my purse and tote behind the counter and invited Captain Moe to join me in the sit-and-stitch square.

He grinned. "I'm looking forward to seeing you sit down in that skirt. I'm not sure you can do it."

"I can manage. Watch." I perched on the edge of one of the club chairs. "See?"

"Danged if you can't." Captain Moe had always reminded me of an older, bearded version of Alan Hale Jr., who had played the Skipper on *Gilligan's Island*. "Are you going to let me in on why you're so dressed up for a workday?"

I took a deep breath. "Captain Moe, do you think I'm the kind of girl men merely flirt with or the kind they fall in love with and marry?"

"Sweet little Marcy, if I were thirty years younger, I'd drop to one knee and ask you to marry me this very instant."

"And if you were only twenty years younger, I'd accept," I said with a smile.

"What's got you doubting yourself?" he asked.

"I suddenly feel very much alone. When I first moved to Tallulah Falls, I was surrounded by activity and people—and, yes, men who appeared interested in me. That has waned recently. Ted is terribly busy with his job. Todd is—" I broke off.

"Under investigation for murder, for one thing," Captain Moe finished. "I think our wee pixie is feeling sorry for herself because she isn't the center of attention these days."

I blushed guiltily. Captain Moe always calls things as he sees them, and he's one of the wisest men on the central coast.

"That is petty, isn't it? I shouldn't be so self-indulgent when my friends' very lives are on the line," I said.

"Ah, no matter," he said jocularly. "We're all entitled to a bit of selfishness now and then. And you're sure to grab headlines today. Why, for fun, you could walk down the street and see how many traffic accidents you can cause."

I laughed at his good-natured ribbing. "I deserve that."

"Yes, you do, Tink. By the way, where's your Jeep and my pal Angus?"

"The Jeep has a dead battery. I called someone before I left the house, so it should soon be as good as new." I frowned. "You mentioned the murder investigation. . . . Did you know Graham?"

"I can tell you that in a way I felt sorry for the man. Graham had no true friends. One reason for that is because he never understood how to be a friend," Captain Moe said. "So the people he thought were his friends either merely tolerated him or were around because they were indebted to him or they wanted something from him."

"Who would gain financially by Graham's death?" I asked.

"That, I don't know. I would imagine his

parents, since he was unmarried and had no children . . . at least, none that he claimed."

"None that he claimed," I mused. "Are you talking about Tawny Milligan's pregnancy?"

He nodded. "I know she was pregnant when she left Tallulah Falls, and most people believed the child to be Graham's. He denied it and very publicly dragged her name through the mud."

"Did you know her?" I asked. "Was she beautiful? I've heard so much talk about her, I'm becoming as obsessed with her as Joan Fontaine was with the first Mrs. de Winter in *Rebecca*."

"She wasn't all that special," he said with a chuckle. "She simply had a way of observing and manipulating people . . . rather like the first Mrs. de Winter." He winked. "It was a horrible skill that Tawny was sometimes able to use to her advantage, but with Graham I believe she used it to her detriment."

"But if Graham was the father of Tawny's child, the child would now be entitled to a portion of Graham's estate, right?"

"If paternity could be proven, then, of course, the mother could petition the court on behalf of her child." He squinted at me. "Are you trying to come up with a plausible motive for murder?"

I grinned. "Of course I am. . . . I'd like to find anything more believable than the idea that Blake or Todd shot him." I sighed. "I want Ted to succeed in finding Graham Stott's killer, but I don't want his testimony to convict Todd or Blake. Right now, it seems that's all he's got." I leaned toward Captain Moe. "You've known everybody in this town a lot longer than I have. Do you think it's possible that Todd or Blake could actually be guilty of Graham's murder?"

Captain Moe took my hands. "Anything is possible. Never close your mind to something, no matter how improbable it may seem. That's when you find yourself in trouble."

Todd walked into the shop then. "Am I interrupting anything?"

Captain Moe stood, deftly pulling me to my feet with him. I was grateful I didn't have to struggle to stand in the skirt. And Captain Moe knew it. He grinned at me with the knowledge of a man who has been around and indulged women for a lifetime. He then looked at Todd. "You're only interrupting an old man's flight of fancy."

I kissed Captain Moe on the cheek. "Oops!" I'd left a bright red lip print. "Let me get a tissue."

"Don't you dare," Captain Moe said. "I'll

wear it with pride. And I'll talk with you again later, my dear." He winked and left the shop.

"Isn't he wonderful?" I asked with a laugh.

"You . . . you look incredible," Todd said. "Is it a special occasion?"

"Nope."

He merely stood there staring at me. "I know it's not your birthday. . . . Is it?"

"What's a birthday?" I smiled. "Is there something you needed?"

"Uh . . . I didn't see the Jeep," he said. "Did you have car trouble this morning?"

"Dead battery." I knew he wanted to ask how I got to work, but he thought it was too impolite to ask. Naturally, I was stubborn enough not to volunteer the information.

"I was headed to MacKenzies' Mochas for an espresso," he said. "Can I bring you something?"

"A latte would be nice."

He nodded, still staring at me with a look of combined admiration and bewildered confusion. "I'll be right back." He nearly tripped over a basket of yarn on his way out the door.

It was hard to keep from giggling. Was it possible I'd just needed to throw a little paint on the old barn in order to feel noticed again?

The phone rang, and I stepped over to the

counter to answer it. "Good morning. Thank you for calling the Seven-Year Stitch."

"Good morning, Marcy. It's Charlie. Any new developments on the Stott investigation?"

"The defense attorneys are insisting the police keep searching for the real killer," I said. "That's about it."

"That's typical defense attorney strategy, but it makes for good copy," Charles said. "I'll run a short piece on it. Thanks. I'll be in touch."

As I ended the call, Ted came into the shop.

"Hi. I didn't see—" He broke off.

I walked over to him. "You didn't see what?"

He swallowed. "The . . . the Jeep. I was worried you'd had car trouble."

"It had a dead battery this morning. Everything should be fine by this afternoon. Thank you for asking."

"How'd you get to work?" he asked.

"I took a cab," I said.

He nodded.

"Would you like to sit down?" I asked. I was pleased that his interest seemed to have been rekindled too, but I was kind of hoping he'd say no. Although I'd navigated the club chair pretty well when Captain Moe had been there, I couldn't be sure I'd pull it off so gracefully the next time.

"I'm short on time," he said. "I just wanted to check on you and make sure you're okay."

"I'm terrific," I said with a smile.

"Yes. Yes, you are." His voice had gone husky. I liked it.

"Did you get the ballistics report back?"

"Yeah. It . . . it wasn't a match. Calloway's gun wasn't the murder weapon," he said. "That doesn't make him or MacKenzie innocent, of course. There could be another gun that was disposed of before we arrived."

"Well, if there is, you'll find it," I said.

"You seem to have a lot of confidence in me," said Ted.

"I do."

His eyes dropped to my lips. "I really want to kiss you right now."

From the corner of my eye, I saw Todd walk past the window. "Now isn't the best time." The phrase *too much of a good thing* crossed my mind.

The shop bells jingled, and Todd brought in my latte. He also handed me a MacKenzies' Mochas bag. "I thought you might like a muffin."

"Thanks," I said. "What do I owe you?"

"Nothing. It's on me."

Todd and Ted were staring at each other

when Vera walked in. I was relieved she'd broken the tension.

"Whoo-hoo!" she said. "Get a look at Tallulah Falls' own Marilyn Monroe! And I ain't talking about Jill. What's with the transformation?"

Ted and Todd appeared to be as anxious to hear my response as Vera was.

I shrugged. "I just decided to try something new today. Do you like it?"

Both men nodded.

"I love it," Vera said. "You look marvelous." She turned to the men. "If you boys are only here to gawk, could you come back a little later? I need some help with my ribbon embroidery project."

"Sure," Ted said. "Marcy, I'm glad there's nothing major wrong with your Jeep. If you need a ride anywhere later, be sure and let me know."

"All right," I said. "I appreciate the offer."

"And I'm free if you need to go somewhere," Todd said.

"Thanks." I smiled. "You guys have a wonderful day."

Vera laughed after they left. "You sure rocked their worlds this morning. Was that your intention?"

"Now, Vera, would I do that? I'm just having a little fun."

We both burst out laughing.

That afternoon during my three o'clock lull when the customers had dwindled, I called Reggie. We chatted briefly about Manu, and she confirmed to me that he was expected home tomorrow.

"Have you learned anything about Tawny's mom's catering business?" I asked.

"It went out of business about five years ago when Tawny's mom died," Reggie said. "There was an article about it online at a small Lincoln City daily newspaper. They even ran a photo of Tawny at the cemetery."

I immediately made a mental note to go to the paper's Web site and look that up. I told Reggie about Captain Moe's visit this morning. "He said most everyone believed Tawny's baby belonged to Graham but that he denied it and dragged Tawny's name through the mud. Still, if it *was* Graham's baby, then she might've had a motive to kill him."

"It's a stretch, but it could be worth pursuing."

"I'm becoming more and more convinced

that Tawny Milligan was somehow involved in Graham's death," I said.

After ending the call, I hurried into the office to look up the site. I'd just pulled it up and did a search for A Special Occasion when Sadie came in.

"Marce, where are you?" she called.

"I'll be right there." I minimized the window and went out into the shop.

"Wowza! You're looking particularly hot today," she said.

I laughed. "Uh . . . thanks."

"So that's what has the guys in a tizzy."

"There are guys in tizzies?" I asked.

"No, it's pretty much the same tizzy, and now I know what it is," she said. "Ted called and said he knew I was upset with him at the moment but could I just tell him whether it's your birthday. I told him it wasn't."

"Why would he think it's my birthday?" I asked. "Do I look older?"

"Hear me out," Sadie said. "Todd came back in after bringing your latte and muffin over this morning and asked if I'd brought you to work this morning. I think he was concerned some Casanova had driven you." She cocked her head at my skirt. "How *did* you get to work this morning?"

"I took a cab," I said.

"So, what's up with the new look? It is a permanent thing?"

"Probably not." I shrugged. "I simply wanted to try something new today." I didn't want to tell her it was spawned in part by being compared with Tawny Milligan and found lacking.

"Well, for the record, I think it worked." She grinned and shook her head. "I've got to get back. Blake'll probably be over to take a gander at you later."

As soon as she left, I hurried back to my office and pulled up the article on the death of Mary Milligan, the founder of A Special Occasion catering company. I scrolled down to the photo Reggie had mentioned of Tawny Milligan at the cemetery. Captain Moe had been right. Tawny was attractive, but she wasn't the stunner I'd imagined her to be. There were people standing in the background, and one man looked like Andy.

I copied and pasted the photo into my picture software so I could enlarge it.

Upon closer inspection, I could see that the man *was* Andy. That wasn't so far-fetched, though. He would be inclined to pay his respects at his first love's mother's funeral.

Standing with him was a little boy who appeared to be four or five years old. Could this be the nephew Andy had spoken of? Or was it Tawny Milligan's child?

I called the newspaper and asked if the photographer who'd been given credit for the photo was still on staff. He was. I spoke with him and asked him to send me a color JPEG of that photo.

"I'll be happy to pay you for it," I said.

"No problem," he told me. "I'll send it as soon as I can find it."

Within thirty minutes, I had the color JPEG of the photo. I enlarged it and could see that both Tawny and the child standing with Andy had the same violet eyes.

Chapter Seventeen

I looked at my watch and saw that it was nearly four o'clock. I called Andy's cell phone number, and when he answered, I asked if he could stop by the shop on his way home.

"I have something I want to show you," I said.

"All right," he said. "I'm in my car now, so I should be there in about twenty minutes."

"Great." I saw a customer—she appeared to be a soccer mom in her early to mid-thirties walking up to the door. "I've got to run. See you in a few." I ended the call and greeted the woman as she stepped into the shop.

She narrowed her eyes as she took in my appearance. "Do you watch that show *Mad Men*?"

"No," I said, thinking maybe she wanted a

pattern like one she'd noticed on the show or something. "I've never seen it. Is it good?"

"I haven't seen it either." She gave a little laugh. "I'm usually watching one of the kids' networks. But I know the fashions from that show are really popular, and I thought . . ." She trailed off. "Anyway, I'm looking for a beginning embroidery kit for my daughter. She's twelve, and she's very creative."

"Step right this way, and I'll show you what I've got." I led her over to the embroidery kits. "I have cross-stitch kits that have the pattern stamped onto the fabric—those are good for beginners. And I have ribbon embroidery kits like this one." I picked up a jewelry box kit that had a stamped pattern that was used to make the top of the box.

"That looks a little hard," the mom said. She looked at the box thoughtfully. "But it's really pretty. She'd love it . . . and she'd be so proud."

"Ribbon embroidery is easier than it looks," I assured her. "You can let your daughter try it, and if it's too difficult for her, just bring it back and I'll return your money."

"Really? Thanks."

"Plus, if she runs into any trouble, just bring her by here, and I'll help her with it," I said. "In fact, I have a beginning ribbon embroidery class currently going on, so I've had plenty of practice lately."

"You offer classes too?" she asked.

"I sure do." I took a flyer off the stack on the counter and handed it to her.

"Thank you. I will go ahead and take this kit," she told me. "As I said, my daughter will absolutely love it."

"And if she doesn't, feel free to bring it back."

She paid for her purchase. "You know, I thought you might be a bit eccentric with the way you're dressed and the mannequin standing at the cash register and everything. But you're super-nice . . . and this place is charming."

I laughed. "Thanks. You're sweet to say so. And please spread the word about the shop."

"I will."

As she took her periwinkle bag and headed down the street, I made a mental note to look up this show *Mad Men* to see who the soccer mom thought I was trying to look like. I hoped I wouldn't be appalled when I found out.

I had no more time to contemplate it, though, because Andy arrived. The instant he saw me, his jaw dropped.

"Andy? Are you all right?" I asked.

"I have never been better," he said as he expelled a long breath. "I can't believe you did this for me. I mean, I meant it when I told you yesterday that you resemble Marilyn Monroe, but I didn't intend for you to actually transform yourself into her for me." He pushed his glasses back up on his face. "I mean, I'm totally glad you did. It was unnecessary, but I'm so flattered. I didn't realize you liked me this much."

"Um . . . whoa, cowboy," I said, holding up both hands in front of me as Andy advanced toward me. "I didn't dress this way for you. I was just experimenting with my look this morning, and this is what I came up with."

"Whatever you say." He smiled and shook his head in disbelief. "Oh, would you please sing 'Happy Birthday' to me? You know, the way Marilyn sang it to JFK—all breathless and sexy?"

"No," I said.

"Please. You can just sing the last two lines if you're afraid of someone coming in and interrupting us."

"No!" I hoped my voice held enough conviction to assure him that I was not now—or ever—going to sing "Happy Birthday" to him . . . unless it was his birthday. And then I wouldn't be singing "all breathless and sexy."

He looked around the shop. "Do you have a water fountain? My mouth has gone so dry I can barely speak."

"I'll get you a bottle of water. Stay here."

"Anything you say," he said.

When I returned with the bottle of water, he was standing exactly where I'd left him.

I handed the bottle to Andy, and he drank half of it in one gulp. He lowered the bottle and swiped his arm across his mouth.

"Do you have any idea how many fantasies are running through my head right now?" he asked me.

"Not a clue, and I don't want to know," I said. "I promise you I did not dress this way in order to seduce you." Gee whiz! How was I gonna get myself out of *this* mess?

"Maybe on some subconscious level, you did." He screwed the top back onto the bottle. "Who do you want me to be? Clark Gable? We could play out a scene from *The Misfits*. No, we don't have that much of an age difference. Thank goodness." He grinned. "I've got it. We could be Cherie and Bo from *Bus Stop* . . . or—"

"No, Andy." I held up both hands straight out in front of me like a frazzled traffic cop. "I want us to be you and me. Friends."

"I'm an idiot," he said.

I was relieved that I was finally getting through to him.

"I'm sorry." He took a step closer to me. "Of

course, you want us to be you and me. We aren't role playing. This is real life."

I wanted to agree with him but something in the way he said it combined with the look in his eyes made me think I should disagree. "Look. I want to be *friends* with you. I didn't dress this way to turn your world upside down. I truly didn't."

"But you wanted to make sure I saw you this way," he said. "You made it a point to call me and ask me to stop by."

"To see something I have in my office," I said. "It's a photograph." I led him to my desk.

I sat down at the computer and pulled up the photograph. "Take a look at this. Does the little boy in this photo belong to Tawny?"

"I'm ... not ... not sure I can see it well enough to tell."

I got up and gave him my seat. "Be honest with me, Andy."

"Fine. Yes," he said with a sigh. "That's Drew. He's Tawny's son."

"You were at her mom's funeral," I said. "That sort of surprised me. I mean, I hadn't thought any of the Alpha Sigs had stayed in touch with her."

"She and I stayed in touch. And a few of the others came to express their condolences to her—Mark, Charles, and Todd were there. There might've been others, but those are the three I remember."

"How about Graham?" I asked. "Was he there?"

Andy scoffed. "Are you kidding? He couldn't have cared less if her mother died. He was never interested in her feelings. In fact, he never cared much about anyone's feelings."

"Why did Todd invite him to the party if none of you liked him?"

"You'll have to ask him," Andy said.

"Is Graham Drew's father?" I asked.

"That's another question I don't know the answer to. When Tawny first got pregnant, she said the baby was Graham's but he denied it. He said she only wanted money from him."

I sat down in the chair beside my desk. "Why didn't she get a paternity test?"

He shrugged. "To save herself and, ultimately, Drew the embarrassment, I imagine. I don't think she knew for sure who Drew's father was either."

"Are you and Tawny still in touch?" I asked. "If Graham *was* the father, then Drew is entitled to his share of the estate."

"We aren't in touch anymore." He sighed heavily.

"Do you think there's any way she could be involved in Graham's death? I mean, what if she ran into money problems, confronted Graham about taking care of his child, and maybe they argued. Later, she could've got a gun and come back and shot him."

"That's impossible," Andy said.

"Why? People do crazy things when they're pushed to the edge."

"Tawny didn't. She was killed in a car crash in early January. That's why she and I aren't in touch anymore."

"Andy, I'm so sorry," I said.

"Yeah, me, too. We were best friends. I know that it's unusual for people who've dated or had feelings for each other in the past to use that affection to grow something even stronger, but we did." He slumped in the chair.

"Wait a second. Why didn't you tell me any of this earlier? You told me the other night that she was just a girl who cleaned the frat house."

"I didn't want to get into my feelings for Tawny when I was trying to cultivate a relationship with you. But she loved me—as a friend—and I never stopped loving her." He briefly closed his eyes. "She was married. Did you know that?"

"I didn't."

"She didn't want her husband to know anything about her past, though, so she kept our friendship from him," he said. "We met once or twice a month in secret. Drew has grown up calling me Uncle Andy."

"He's the nephew with the Jack Russell?"

"Yeah." He grinned.

"How about Tawny's husband? Was he someone you knew?"

"I've never met him," Andy said. "Like I told you, she didn't want her old life interfering with her new one."

"Have you seen Drew since his mom died?" I asked.

"Once . . . in February. He was with Tawny's dad and wanted to see me, so Mr. Milligan gave me a call."

"It must be hard," I said. "You're grieving for her. And, in a way, you're grieving for Drew too."

"We still get to stay in touch," said Andy. "We e-mail and Skype and text each other. And I'll probably see him again the next time he comes to see his grandpa."

"That's good." I glanced at the clock and saw that it was after five p.m. "Andy, what kind of car do you drive?"

"A Camaro. Why?"

"They're pretty low to the ground, aren't they?"

He nodded.

"Would you mind giving me a ride home?"

I locked up the shop and put the sign in the window assuring my students I'd be back in time for class. Andy helped me into the passenger seat of his yellow Camaro.

"This is nice," I said.

"Thanks."

We drove most of the way home in silence, except for my giving him directions. When we got there, I told him I'd invite him in to say hi to Angus, but I really needed to change clothes and get back to class.

"That's fine," he said. "Hopefully, I'll see him another time. I know I acted like a total drip earlier. It's just—"

"We'll pretend it never happened," I interrupted.

"Yeah. I know I probably shouldn't even ask, but may I still take you out to dinner tomorrow night?"

"I'd like that," I said.

I dug my keys out of my purse before stepping out of Andy's car. It was so much easier to get into and out of than my Jeep. For a second, it made me rethink my purchase. Still, I knew Angus's toenails would likely damage the leather interior, and he wouldn't have as much room in a sporty little car as he did in the Jeep. While it would sometimes be nice to have either a car or a stepladder, I'd rather have Angus than convenience.

I turned and waved to Andy as I unlocked my door and went inside. The first thing I did was go upstairs and trade in my pencil skirt for a pair of jeans. I kept the sweater and the black pumps, though. I had to admit, it was nice to look and feel feminine. And though I often wore heels to counter my height—or, rather, lack of height—I usually dressed tomboyishly unless it was some sort of special occasion.

I went back downstairs and let Angus in. I fed him, and I ate a bowl of cereal and a piece of toast. I made Angus a piece of toast too. Then, since I'd left Angus home today, I took him back to the shop with me. Thankfully, the Jeep's engine turned over on the first try . . . good as new. The bill I'd be getting in the mail wouldn't be so hot, but at least I had my Jeep back.

As I waited for my students to arrive, I busied myself with the Mountmellick project. I was almost halfway through it, and I was really pleased with how it was turning out. While I worked, I wondered what—if anything—the fact that Tawny was dead would have on the investigation. If Graham was her son's father, then Drew was entitled to a share of his estate unless Graham and Tawny had some sort of legal agreement that Graham would have no financial responsibility for his child's life. While I thought Tawny was living, this had given her an excellent motive to want Graham dead. But didn't Drew's guardian still have motive to want Graham dead? Maybe Tawny's death had left her husband in a bind financially, and he'd been the one to confront Graham about money. They could've argued, and the husband could have taken advantage of the crowd at the Brew Crew to shoot Graham and then slip away unnoticed.

I set my embroidery aside long enough to go back into my office and look up the article about Tawny's mother again. I read it more carefully this time and learned that Tawny's dad's name was John Milligan. He still lived in Lincoln City at the time of his wife's death. I was guessing he was still there because Andy said he'd gone to see Drew in February while the child was with his grandfather.

I searched the white pages and came up with

an address for Mr. Milligan. I decided I'd pay him a visit before coming to work in the morning to see what he could tell me about Graham, Drew, and Tawny's widowed husband.

I heard my students beginning to filter into the shop, and I exited out of the windows I'd opened on my computer and went to greet them. Tonight's class was beginning needlepoint. It was a diverse group—teens, tweens, moms, and grandmothers. And Sadie. I'd finally convinced her to take the class so she could complete the kit I'd given her in October. So what if it was a bear dressed as a pumpkin for Halloween? She'd have it when Halloween rolled around this year.

Angus was thrilled with all the attention he received from the students. Before class got started, they played fetch with him, rubbed his belly, and talked about how adorable he was.

Class went smoothly, and afterward I asked Sadie to stay behind for a second. After everyone else had left, I told her about how I'd found the photo of Tawny and her son and that Andy was in the picture.

"So I called Andy and asked him to come by," I said. "He told me that he didn't know who the father of Tawny's child was, but Captain Moe said almost everyone thought the baby belonged to Graham."

"And this is important because?" Sadie asked.

"Because it provides a motive for Graham's murder. At first I thought maybe the killer was Tawny—that she'd needed money or got sick of Graham not supporting their child or something. But then Andy told me that Tawny had died in a car accident in January of this year."

"So that rules out that theory," she said.

I raised an index finger. "Not necessarily. Tawny was married. Andy doesn't know who she was married to because he never met the guy. Tawny kept their friendship secret because she didn't want her husband to know about her tarnished past."

"So you think the husband could've killed Graham? For money?"

"Stranger things have happened," I said.

"Stranger than what?" Blake asked.

Sadie and I were in my office and hadn't noticed the bells signal Blake's arrival. She told him about my discovery, my conversation with Andy, and my latest theory.

"Who did Tawny marry?" Blake asked.

"Andy didn't know," I said.

"Well . . . I hope she was happy," he said softly.

Sadie frowned at him. "You sound a little sentimental there."

"Eh, she was a nice girl. She deserved better than she got from Graham," Blake said.

"Did you know her well?" Sadie asked.

"We dated for a brief time," he admitted.

"How come you never told me that?" Sadie clamped her lips together in a firm line.

Meanwhile, I wished I was somewhere else. Or at least invisible. This was a private moment between a wife and her husband, and I didn't need to be witnessing it.

"Babe, please," said Blake. "That was a lifetime ago. Let's just allow the past to be the past, all right?"

Sadie said okay, but the strain was evident on her face when they left. I hoped it was simply because she was tired. I mean, she'd been through a *lot* the past few days, and this had to be one more straw on that poor camel's back. I'd call and check on her after I got to work in the morning . . . and maybe tell her what I'd been able to find out—if anything—from Mr. Milligan.

Chapter Eighteen

On Friday morning, I dressed more sensibly than I had the day before. Today's outfit consisted of jeans, sneakers, and a long-sleeved T-shirt. I fed Angus and put him outside with the promise that I'd come back to get him before I went in to work. I grabbed a protein bar and a Diet Coke, went out to the Jeep, and punched in the address for John Milligan. I then started the approximately half-hour drive to Lincoln City.

When I got to John Milligan's house, he was sitting on his porch in a sweatshirt and running pants. I pulled up to the curb and got out.

Mr. Milligan was reading the newspaper and drinking a cup of coffee. He had thick gray hair that was kind of wavy, and when he looked up at me, I could see that he, too, had those violet eyes.

"Good morning," I said.

"How are you, young lady?" He put the paper aside. "Can I help you with something?"

"Are you Mr. Milligan?"

He nodded.

"I came by partly to express my condolences on the loss of your daughter. I only found out about her accident yesterday." I took a step toward the porch, and he invited me to come on up and sit down.

"You knew Tawny?" he asked.

"No, I'm afraid I didn't—but several of my friends did: Todd Calloway, Blake MacKenzie, Riley Kendall. . . ." I sat down on the wrought-iron chair beside him.

"Are you here about Tawny or that business about Graham Stott getting shot last week?" His tone took on a less friendly tone.

"I'm actually here about Drew," I said. "I started looking into Graham's past because I wanted to help my friends. I don't think they're guilty of murder."

He shrugged. "If they are, they did the world a favor, in my opinion. But I can't help you."

I let his comment pass. "If Graham was Drew's biological father, even if Graham denied paternity while he was living, Drew is entitled to a portion of his estate. And I think the boy should have it."

"Drew doesn't need any of Graham Stott's filthy money," Mr. Milligan said.

"Well, not now, maybe, but it would be good for Drew to have for college or for some unexpected emergency." I looked into Mr. Milligan's violet eyes. "I'm not trying to meddle. But it appears to me that Graham treated your daughter horribly, and her son deserves to be compensated for that."

He offered me a slight smile. "I believe your heart is in the right place, miss. But even though Tawny named Graham as the child's father on the birth certificate, he wasn't."

I frowned. "Why did she say he was, then?"

"She wanted him to be," he said. "And I believe she honestly thought the child was his at first." He dropped his head. "She loved Graham so much. She thought the baby would bring them together . . . and that even though Graham had denied the baby was his initially, that when he saw the boy, he'd know . . . and that he'd love the child and maybe Tawny too . . . and that they'd all live happily ever after. She was such a dreamer."

"I'm sorry it didn't work out that way," I

told him. "Did Tawny make Graham take a paternity test? Or did she simply give up when he remained firm in his denial?"

"Graham didn't need to take a paternity test," Mr. Milligan said, raising his eyes to mine again. "After she gave birth to the child, Tawny called Graham and asked him to come and see his son. Graham came, all right, but it wasn't with flowers and declarations of love. It was with his medical records and an attorney. The medical records proved Graham had been sterile since being injured in a dirt bike accident when he was twelve. The attorney provided a legal injunction forbidding Tawny to use Stott as the boy's last name."

"I'm so very sorry," I said.

He smiled sadly. "Me, too. My baby girl was heartbroken. After that, she changed her name to Sarah, and she and her son used the surname Masterson—it was my mother's maiden name. And then Tawny took the boy and moved to Portland."

"That couldn't have been easy for you or your wife."

"It wasn't. We felt a little better about her after she married," said Mr. Milligan. "Charlie was a good man she'd also known in school, and he had become a newspaper reporter and was doing well for himself."

"Wait," I said. "She married Charles? Charles Siegel?" No way. It had to be a different Charlie who was a reporter in Portland.

"Yes. Do you know Charles?" he asked.

"Not very well. I met him through Todd Calloway recently. But I had no idea he was married to your daughter." I frowned. "Is it possible that *he* is Drew's father?"

"No. The two of them didn't get together until Drew was a couple years old," he said. "Charlie loves the boy as if he's his own, though."

"That's wonderful," I said, wondering why on earth Charles had decided not to mention his relationship with Tawny. "And it's good Drew has his uncle Andy in his life too."

"Yeah." Mr. Milligan smiled. "Andy stuck by Tawny through thick and thin. And he stays in touch with Drew even now. There were times when I wished Tawny would have married Andy. Anyone with eyes in his head could see how much Andy loved her." He lifted and dropped his shoulders. "But she wound up with Charles, and he loved her too. And she loved him. It worked out for the best. It seems you're acquainted with all Tawny's old friends."

"It does seem that way," I said. "I wish I could've known her too."

I stopped by the library on my way back through Tallulah Falls to talk with Reggie. I didn't know what to make of this new development, and I wanted her input.

The library was housed in a beautiful brick Victorian building about a mile outside of Tallulah Falls. Upon opening the main door, there was a cozy seating area to the right that contained two weathered leather sofas and some overstuffed chairs. I went into the room to my left where the circulation desk was located.

"Hi, I'm here to see Reggie Singh," I said to the fresh-faced young woman manning the desk.

She dialed Reggie's extension on an intercom and told her I was there. "She said to go on back. Do you know where her office is?"

"I do. Thanks." I walked down the narrow hallway, glad I wasn't wearing heels today to clack on the hardwood floor. I tapped on Reggie's semi-closed door, and she asked me to come on in.

Reggie's office was one of the most eclectically decorated I'd ever seen, and yet, it worked.

Indian influences mixed with coastal photographs to create a pleasantly exotic look. Actually, Reggie herself had a pleasantly exotic look. Today she wore a pink beaded tunic with matching slacks and a white pashmina. The gold hoop earrings she wore set off her face, which was framed by her salt-and-pepper pixie-cut hair.

I sat down on the armless Victorian silk-covered armchair beside Reggie's desk. "This murder investigation just keeps getting crazier and crazier. When I think I have a motive and a potential suspect, everything flips and I've got nothing."

"So, who's flipped?" she asked.

I relayed the story about seeing who I believed to be Tawny's child in the photograph with Andy, calling Andy, and having him stop by the office. "I thought Tawny had the perfect motive for murdering Graham, but then Andy told me Tawny was dead. So I paid a visit to Tawny's dad this morning."

Reggie frowned. "You thought maybe her *dad* had killed Graham?"

"No, but that is a thought . . . or, at least, it *would* have been if what I'd thought when I went to see Mr. Milligan had been true. You see, I believed Tawny's child had an inheritance coming to him and that he should have it. Mr. Milligan let me know in no uncertain terms that there's no way Graham Stott was the father of Tawny's baby because Graham was sterile."

"Really?" Reggie turned down the corners of her mouth. "That's something I wouldn't imagine a man would want to advertise. I'd have thought that, given his position and money, Graham would have rather said the baby was his than to have owned up to being sterile."

"I don't think he did own up to it until push actually came to shove," I said. "Mr. Milligan said Graham even brought a lawyer to forbid Tawny to use the Stott name for the child. That's when she changed her name, gave the baby the last name Masterson, and left town. And get this! She went to Portland, and two years down the road, she married Charles Siegel!"

"And this Siegel news has you particularly vexed because . . ."

"Because I've been giving him information about the trial in exchange for information about Graham," I told her. "He barely talked about Tawny at all, and he certainly never mentioned that he'd married her and was raising her child."

"Maybe he thought it wasn't relevant," said Reggie.

"Maybe not, but you can bet I'm going to ask him about it. All along I've been thinking Graham's murder *had* to have something to do with Tawny Milligan or the baby she'd had. Now I'm back to square one, and I don't have a single thing to go on."

Reggie placed her hand lightly over mine. "Marcy, let the police do their jobs. This is not your responsibility. You have plenty to do without getting stressed-out over this."

When I started to protest, she held up her hand.

"I know Sadie and Blake and Todd are your friends," she continued. "But the police want justice as badly as you do. Besides, Manu will be back home tonight. Maybe having someone look at the matter with fresh eyes will give the investigation an entirely new perspective."

"Thanks, Reggie. I hope you're right."

Even though I hurried home to get Angus and we drove straight back to the shop, I was a few minutes late opening the store. Plus, when we got there, I noticed that the deliveryman had come and gone and had left a huge box outside the door.

I parked the Jeep, got Angus out, and took

him inside. I put my purse and tote on the counter and went back outside to wrestle the box into the shop.

As soon as I bent to try to pick up the box, I heard someone say, "Stop."

I turned and saw Mark hurrying toward me with a to-go cup from MacKenzies' Mochas.

"Tell me you were not about to try and pick up that box that way," he said.

"Actually, that's exactly what I was about to do." I smiled. "You're here in the nick of time."

"I'll say. Let me set this cup down." He went into the Seven-Year Stitch and placed his cup on the counter.

Angus bounded over, and Mark gave him a quick pat on the head before coming back outside.

"All right. Let me show you how to do this," he said.

"Okay." I was still smiling. All my talk about not wanting to be a damsel in distress flew right out the window when I had a heavy box to move and a strong guy around to move it.

"If you're going to try and pick up a box this size, you bend with your knees. That way you use your legs to help lift and take the pressure off your back." He stooped and properly picked up the box.

"Fantastic!" I opened the door.

Mark put the box back down exactly where he'd got it. "Now you try it."

My smile went away. Far, far away. I had a bodybuilder at my disposal and he was *not* going to pick up my measly little box and carry it into my shop for me? What was up with that?

I rubbed my hands down the sides of my jeans. I'd *try* to pick it up—the proper way—and when he saw that I wasn't strong enough, *then* he'd bring it inside for me.

I bent at the knees, wrapped my arms around the box and stood. I was able to pick it up, but I nearly dropped it and put it back down. Did I mention this box was *huge*? I looked at Mark. Surely he'd get it for me now.

"You almost had it," he said. "Try it again. This time get your arms under it a little better."

I stared at him. It was almost a glare, but I tried to temper it. This barbarian was setting back chivalry a thousand years!

I wiped my hands on my jeans again, bent, and picked up the box. I'd get that stupid box into the shop or bust. I'd show him I didn't need his help. I got up under the box, lifted it, and—when Mark opened the door for me—carried it into the shop. I rushed to the counter and set the box down.

I turned to Mark triumphantly. "How'd you like that?"

"I loved it," he said. "How did *you* like it?"

I grinned slowly. "I think I loved it, too . . . not at first, but . . . yeah, I feel good about being about to carry it in here myself."

"Good." He smiled. "When I was showing you how to pick it up, I was also testing its weight. If I'd thought you'd hurt yourself bringing it in, I'd have done it for you. I knew you could handle that box."

"Thank you. If you hadn't pushed me, I wouldn't have done it."

"That's what a personal trainer does," said Mark.

"Can you believe it's been a week since Graham was killed?" I asked, trying to find a way to draw him into a conversation about the shooting. "Have they scheduled his funeral yet?"

"I haven't heard," he said. "I do know he has family that lives out of town, so maybe the service has been postponed until they get here."

"Maybe. Prolonging the funeral and the closure it would provide is bound to be hard for his parents, though. But I guess it's good he doesn't have any children or anything." I watched Mark's face, but he was giving nothing away. "I'd heard he fathered a child with Tawny Milligan, but that turned out to be just a rumor."

"I'd always heard her baby belonged to Graham, but I never gave it much thought," he said. "I feel sorry for the child, though. He's what now? Ten?"

"I imagine so."

Mark shook his head. "And he's growing up without a father."

"Well, not totally, from what I can understand. Tawny married Charles Siegel, and he's been like a father to the boy," I said.

"It's not the same," Mark said. "I grew up with plenty of uncles and cousins. But my dad wasn't around. That was tough. I always felt like he hadn't wanted me. If he had, he'd have been around."

"You don't seem at all surprised that Tawny and Charles were married."

"I know more than a lot of people give me credit for knowing. I just don't talk about what I know or what I don't know. I learned a long time ago not to go poking my nose around in other people's business . . . especially if I didn't want them poking around in mine." He gave me a pointed look. "Messing in other people's business is a good way to get yourself shot in the back room of a bar."

Long after Mark had left, I kept mulling over what he'd said. He was definitely warning me. Did he know who'd really killed Graham Stott? Did he know the identity of Drew's father? As far as I knew, the father could be Roberto, Andy, Charles—despite what John Milligan thought—or Blake. Todd had said he didn't think Blake would have slept with Tawny while he was dating Sadie, but he hadn't sounded very sure of that. And Sadie had been upset last night to learn that Blake had dated Tawny and hadn't mentioned it to her.

What if Blake was the father of Tawny's child? Granted, he dated Tawny before he ever met Sadie. But could he have hooked up with Tawny in a moment of weakness? And if so, would Sadie ever forgive him for giving another woman a child when they'd had so much trouble conceiving? I tried to put the thought out of my head. That baby *had* to belong to someone other than Blake.

Chapter Nineteen

When I had a break between customers that morning, I called Charles.

"I didn't expect to hear back from you so soon," he said. "Have there been some new developments in the investigation?"

"Not really," I said, trying to keep my voice sounding casual. "I'm just wondering why you didn't tell me you were married to Tawny Milligan."

He was silent for a moment before saying, "I wasn't married to Tawny Milligan. I was married to Sarah Masterson. Sarah and I had left Tawny far in the past. Besides, my personal life is none of your business."

"I agree. But I learned about your wife's

passing, and I am sorry for your loss and for your son's loss," I said.

"How did you hear about Sarah's death?" Charles asked.

"I'd been trying to find her because I thought she might know of someone who could have wanted to kill Graham," I said.

"Why would she know anything about that?" he asked. "Even if she was still living, she hadn't seen the man in a decade."

"True, but it was widely believed that Graham was the father of her child. I figured she would have kept up with him." I took a deep breath before dropping another bomb. "Up until I found out Tawny—or Sarah—was dead, I thought she might have had something to do with Graham's murder."

"Where are you getting your information?" he asked tersely.

"I went to see Tawny's father. Mr. Milligan—"

"You intruded on a grieving father?" Charles interrupted. "You've got a lot of nerve."

"Had I known about your marriage to Tawny, I wouldn't have gone. I didn't know at that time that Drew had a dad in his life, and I thought Mr. Milligan might want to petition the court for whatever inheritance the child had coming from Graham's estate," I said.

"What's it to you?"

"Graham Stott treated your wife like dirt, and I thought he should pay for it! And I wanted to make sure her child was provided for."

He sighed. "He *did* treat Sarah poorly, but as I told you, we put the past as far behind us as we could get it."

"Then what were you doing at a party with Graham?" I asked.

"I didn't know he'd be there. None of us really liked him—a few of the guys tolerated him at best." He paused. "What else did John tell you?"

"He told me Graham wasn't Drew's father."

"Did he tell you who is?" Charles asked.

"No," I said. "He didn't know. Is it you?"

"I am now. That's all that matters," he said quietly.

"That *is* all that matters. I'm glad he's got you." I was thinking *And Andy,* but I didn't say that. Andy had made it clear that Tawny's husband hadn't known about their friendship, and Charles had made it clear that he thought his wife had cut all ties to her past.

"You take a lot on yourself, you know that?" he asked. "You should really leave the detective work to those trained to do it, Ms. Singer. They're a lot more capable than you are."

"I don't doubt their expertise," I said. "But I believe my friends are innocent, and I'll do whatever I can to help prove it and to find out who really killed Graham Stott. Do you have any theories as to who shot him?"

"Yes, I have one—the only plausible one there is. Graham was killed by either Todd Calloway, Blake MacKenzie, or both of them. I'm not sure which one pulled the trigger, but you can bet one of them did. You can't mix old grudges with liquor and expect a pleasant outcome. My advice to you is to stop wasting everybody's time—including your own—and put your energy into throwing your buddies a going-away party."

"I'm sorry you feel that way," I said.

"I suppose our so-called partnership is off," he said. "Just so you know, the Seven-Year Stitch is being featured in Sunday's edition of the paper. So I figure we're square for the information you've provided to date."

"I guess we are," I said.

I ended the call, went into the storeroom, closed the door, and screamed into a bolt of fabric. This, naturally, made Angus bark at the door because he wondered what was making me scream. The next thing I knew, Todd was flinging open the storeroom door.

"What's wrong?" he asked. "I came in and saw Angus having a fit at the door and was afraid you might be hurt or something."

"Not so much hurt. Just furious." I put the bolt of fabric back onto the shelf and left the storeroom. "Why do you always catch me at my worst?"

"I wouldn't say that," Todd said. He followed me out and closed the door.

We went into the sit-and-stitch area and both sat down on the sofa facing the window.

"Do you want to talk about it?" he asked.

"Yes and no. I just had an argument with Charles Siegel. I'd initially hoped he could provide information about the shooting, so I agreed to send him information about the trial and investigation in exchange for publicity for the Seven-Year Stitch." I threw my head against the back of the sofa and closed my eyes. "Then I found out that he was married to Tawny Milligan, who had changed her name to Sarah Masterson, and that he is raising her child."

"He and Tawny were married? When did that happen? And why is *he* raising the child? Where is she?" Todd asked.

"She's dead. She was killed in a car accident in January," I said.

"Oh, man."

I raised my head and looked at Todd. "I'm sorry. I didn't intend that to come out so abruptly. I'd forgotten the two of you were friends."

"It's all right," he said. "Finish your story."

"Charles got angry that I was poking into his wife's business, and he insisted that the police have the right people in custody." I folded one leg under me. "See, all roads kept leading back to Tawny Milligan. All of you knew her, many of you had dated her, and she left town supposedly carrying Graham's child. And when Graham found out she was pregnant, he treated her like dirt. I thought if anyone had a motive to want him dead, it was her."

"But why would you think she'd wait ten years to get her revenge?" Todd asked.

"I thought maybe she or the child needed money for some reason. I'd decided that maybe Tawny had gone to Graham, asked him to do the right thing, he refused, and she thought she'd have a better chance at getting what she needed from him if he was dead." I spread my hands. "If the father wouldn't give the child money while he was living, maybe she could get it from his estate."

"Graham wasn't the father."

"I know that *now*," I said. "Of course, I had to find out from her *dad* because no one else volunteered the information. How did you know Graham wasn't the father?"

"He had a dirt bike accident when he was twelve. I was with him." Todd smiled sadly to himself. "He told me afterwards that he couldn't get a girl pregnant anymore. And he was thrilled. He was too young to consider the seriousness of that."

"At twelve, he was happy he couldn't get a girl pregnant?" I asked.

"We were seeing all the sex ed films in school. He was looking ahead." He shrugged. "Just stupid kid talk."

"Who was the father of Tawny's baby?" I asked softly.

"I don't know," he said.

"You don't know, or you don't want to tell me?"

He turned his head slowly toward me. "It isn't me."

"I didn't think it was. Is it Blake?" I asked.

He lowered his eyes. "I doubt it."

"You doubt it, but you don't know for sure."

"It doesn't matter," he said. "That's ancient history. Digging in it now would only jeopardize Blake's marriage to Sadie."

I ran my hands through my hair in frustration. "Why in the world did you have to invite

Graham Stott to that stupid party? You knew how much animosity there was between him and most of the other Alpha Sigs. Was it because he'd given you money when you first opened the Brew Crew?"

"No. He offered me money, but I didn't take it. I didn't want to be indebted to Graham Stott . . . or to anyone else, for that matter," said Todd. "I invited Graham because I felt sorry for him. I wanted to try to get back the friendship we'd had when we were kids."

"Look how that worked out for you. You're getting ready to stand trial for his murder," I said. "And someone else who was in the Brew Crew last Friday night—maybe another of your Alpha Sig brothers—is more than happy to stand by and let you and Blake take the blame." I was so angry that I was a little out of control. "The two of you need to start helping the police figure out who killed Graham, or else you're going to be serving life sentences in prison!"

Todd's chocolate-colored eyes narrowed, and his jaw clenched. "Are you doubting the valiant Detective Nash? Do you no longer think your hero can swoop in and save the day?"

"I believe Ted is an excellent detective, but he didn't know Graham Stott. You and Blake did, and you'd better start feeding Ted some possible leads. Take responsibility for your life, Todd!"

"Fine." He got up and strode out the door.

Angus peeped timidly out from behind the other sofa.

I heaved a deflated sigh. "It's all right, baby."

He trotted over and sat down at my feet. I kissed the top of his head and gave him a hug. It's wonderful to have a friend who always loves you no matter what.

Later that afternoon I was restocking monk's cloth, Aida fabric, and items (such as towels, baby bibs, and blankets) with spaces for embroidering. The phone rang, and it was Mom.

"You might not want to talk with me today," I warned her. "I've made everyone else I've talked to angry."

"Oh, darling, you could never make me angry," she said.

"And you shouldn't lie. At least, that's what you always told me."

"Okay, so you can make me angry. I'll take my chances. What have you done to everyone else?" she asked.

"It's this stupid murder investigation."

"Which you should probably not be involved

in, but that's beside the point," Mom said. "I know you can't help yourself. Please continue."

I told her about how I'd been so sure this Tawny Milligan had been involved with the murder somehow, especially since I found out she was pregnant presumably with Graham Stott's child when she left Tallulah Falls. "But now I don't know *who* the father is—not that it has any bearing on this investigation at this point—and I've wasted my time chasing leads that don't matter. And, on top of that, I made Todd angry this morning by telling him he needed to take responsibility for his life and help the police find out who really killed Graham."

"Well, he *does* need to take the wheel on this, darling. You were right. And as for Tawny, don't count out the vengeance of a woman scorned even from the grave," Mom said. "Remember that movie I worked on, *Vengeance from the Grave*?"

"I remember." And, unfortunately, I did. That movie had been a real stinker. "But I don't think Tawny Milligan came back as a zombie and shot Graham Stott."

"That's beside the point. All I'm saying is that just because Tawny's child didn't belong to Graham doesn't mean that the Alpha Sigs' past didn't factor into the shooting," she said.

"Now, granted, it could've been a random thing carried out by a stranger, but I doubt it. Sometimes old resentments fester until they simply explode with no further warning."

"I guess that's true. But, Mom, what if Blake is the father of Tawny Milligan's child?" I asked.

"If he is, then what he'll do about it is up to him, love. And it will be up to Sadie to decide whether or not she cares about him enough to stand by him no matter what he decides. If it'll make you feel better, talk with Blake privately and ask him if he thinks it's possible the boy is his. He might not have even considered it a possibility."

After we hung up, I called MacKenzies' Mochas. I'd already decided that if Sadie answered, I'd tell her I'd made Todd angry and ask her whether she thought I should give him some space or try to make up. If Blake answered, I could ask him to come over and talk with me when he got a chance. Fortunately for me, Blake answered.

"Hi," I said. "How's it going?"

"Okay. You need Sadie?" he asked.

"No, actually, I want to talk with you. Privately. Could you come to the shop when you get time?" I asked.

"Yeah." He drew the word out. "What's up?"

"I'll explain when you get here."

While I waited for Blake to arrive, I worked on the Mountmellick piece. I was couching the petals of a daisy when he walked in.

His face showed his concern as he looked around the shop to see what might be wrong.

"Please come and sit down with me," I said as Angus bounded over to Blake to be petted.

"Okay." He patted Angus absently and came to sit on the red club chair opposite me. "What's going on, Marce? You're freaking me out."

"Is there any possibility you could be the father of Tawny Milligan's child?"

He ran his hand over the lower portion of his face. "Why are you asking me about that?"

I explained that after I'd learned about Tawny's pregnancy and shoddy treatment by Graham, that I was convinced Graham was the father of her child and that she'd been involved in his shooting. "But then I found out Graham wasn't the father of Tawny's baby."

"I repeat—why are you asking me about it?"

"Because if you are, I thought you—and Drew—had the right to know," I told him. "You don't have to do anything about it if he *is* your son, but I thought you should know in case he is."

His jaw worked, and he gripped the arms of the chair.

"Say something," I said at last.

"Um, all righty." Sarcasm dripped from his voice. "I'll jump up from here and rush down the street to tell my wife—with whom I've been trying unsuccessfully to father a child— that I might already have a son by another woman. She'll be ever so delighted!"

"So you're thinking Drew *is* yours?" I asked.

"I don't know what to think. Could a one-night stand with Tawny Milligan when I was on a break with Sadie result in a child? Possibly. Could it destroy my marriage if Sadie ever finds out? Definitely." He stood. "I've got to get out of here and clear my head. If Sadie calls, tell her I had to run an errand. I'll think up something to tell her later."

Fantastic. More lies.

I needed to do something to fix this. I didn't want to be responsible for Blake and Sadie's marriage falling apart. Although, technically, the events that would be responsible for that wouldn't be *my* fault, but I'd be the one who set the revelation of them in motion.

I called Charles Siegel. When he answered, I quickly asked him to please not hang up.

"What is it?" he asked impatiently.

"Is Blake MacKenzie Drew's biological father?" I asked.

"Why don't you ask him that?"

"I did," I admitted. "He says it's possible. But I thought that maybe your wife had told you the truth, and I'm praying the father is someone other than Blake."

"Marcy, why do you keep prying into this?" His voice sounded plaintive.

"I don't know. I honestly wish I hadn't. I just thought that if there was any way Blake could be the father, he should know he had a child in the world," I said. "And that Drew might need his biological father sometime too. I mean, what if Drew had some sort of physical condition, or . . ."

"You're stretching," he said gently. "My wife went through a time of confusion and experimentation when she was younger. To put it another way, she sowed her wild oats." He sighed. "She wasn't sure who the father of her baby was. Tell Blake to let it go."

"I wish I could."

"What do you mean?" His tone had lost its gentleness and now had an edge to it.

"I just talked with Blake about it, and he rushed out of here," I said. "I don't know where he went."

Chapter Twenty

I spent the next couple of hours leaving messages on Blake's cell phone, working on the Mountmellick piece, waiting on customers, and feeling rotten. When Ted walked in at about two thirty and asked how I was doing, I burst into tears.

He rushed to my side and gathered me into his arms. "Marcy, what is it?"

"I should never have gotten involved in this murder investigation. I should've trusted you and the rest of the crime team to do your jobs." I gulped. "But I was afraid nobody else believed Blake and Todd were innocent, and now I don't have any friends anymore, and I've probably destroyed Blake and Sadie's marriage." I ended on a wracking sob.

Ted kissed my temple while Angus simultaneously licked my ankle.

"Come on," Ted said in a soothing voice. "It's not all that bad, is it? You've still got Angus and me."

"It's awful, Ted. I've messed everything up. I meddled where I didn't have any business, and it only stirred up a lot of trouble. It didn't even help anything."

"Don't be so hard on yourself. You always meddle where you don't have any business. This situation can't be any worse than some of the others you've found yourself in."

I pushed back to look up at him indignantly.

"What?" he asked with mock naïveté. "I was only trying to help." He pulled me back into his embrace.

I nestled against him, wishing I could stay hidden in his arms until all this mess had resolved itself . . . in a miraculously good way.

Ted must have felt me relax, because he decided this was a good opportunity to tease me. "Yesterday I came in here and found Marilyn Monroe. Today, it was Lucy Ricardo."

I chuckled. "Which one did you like the best . . . or do I even have to ask?"

"I like Marcy Singer the best," he said. "I've missed that young woman."

"She's missed you," I said.

"You wanna talk about what made you have a meltdown now that you're feeling better?" Ted asked.

"Not really. Just tell me you're considering other leads in the case and that you aren't convinced that Blake and Todd killed Graham."

"All right. I'm considering other leads in the case because I'm not entirely convinced that Blake and Todd killed Graham." He paused. "How was that?"

"Did you mean it?"

"I meant it." His voice had both deepened and softened. He either meant it, or he was trying really, really hard to make me feel better.

"Thank you." I sat back so I could look into Ted's clear blue eyes.

He grabbed a tissue from the coffee table and wiped the mascara from beneath my eyes. "We don't want some customer coming in and thinking you're the president of the Alice Cooper fan club."

"How do you know I'm not?" I asked. "By the way, welcome to my nightmare."

"If I have my way about it, you'll be having sweet dreams again before you know it." He smiled. "By the way, are you free for dinner on Sunday?"

"Yes, as a matter of fact, I am."

"I'm glad. Pick you up at six?" he asked.

"That sounds great."

As soon as Ted had left, I hurried to the bathroom to wash my face and put on fresh makeup. It was a good thing I kept a makeup kit in my office. It had certainly come in handy this week. I was putting the finishing touches on my face when I heard the shop door's bells jingle. I half hoped it was Blake, but I half hoped it was anyone else . . . other than Sadie. I called that I'd be right out.

"Take your time," Vera called. Her voice became a falsetto. "How's my handsome boy? How is he? Does he like his new toy? Hmm? Oh, you're such a sweet baby."

I stepped into the shop and saw that Vera had taken a seat on the sofa, and Angus was sitting at her feet with his head in her lap.

"Angus," I chided gently. "I doubt Vera wants long gray hairs all over her clothes."

"Now, you leave him alone," she said. "He's just fine." She reached into her tote bag and brought out her ribbon embroidery project she was working on. "I need some help with these infernal spider-web roses. I can't do them right to save my life."

I sat down beside her. "Let me see you make one."

I watched as she carefully outlined the "spider web" or "wagon wheel" with yellow embroidery thread. She then took her yellow satin ribbon and began working it through the spokes.

"Slow down," I said.

She looked up. "What?"

"Don't work so quickly. With ribbon embroidery, you have to take your time. Pull the ribbon slowly and more gently to make it come through properly without going too far."

"I get impatient," she said.

"I know. But try it almost like you're in slow motion from your normal speed." I had to stifle a giggle as Vera took "slowly and gently" to the extreme. But her rose looked beautiful when she'd finished. "See?"

She smiled. "Yes, I do! That looks fantastic!"

"It does. Now make another."

She made another, this time picking up the pace a little but still slower than she'd been earlier. Again the rose looked great.

"I'm getting the hang of this," Vera said. As she used the embroidery floss to prepare to make another rose, she asked, "Did your romantic rivals opt for pistols or swords yesterday?"

"What?" I asked.

"When I came in yesterday afternoon, I thought Todd and Ted were going to engage in a duel right then and there." She sighed wistfully. "I remember when young men looked at me the way those two were looking at you. It's wonderful, isn't it?"

"Well, I don't know that I'll be looked at that way again by Todd anytime soon," I said. "I made him angry this morning. Ted did ask me to go to dinner with him Sunday, though." I decided I'd much rather talk about her. "How about your newspaper guy, Paul? Did you enjoy dinner with him the other night?"

"I did, dear. He and I had a wonderful time. After dinner, he took me dancing at the Starlight Room in the Tallulah Falls Tavern," she said. "Have you been there yet?"

"No, I haven't." It seemed more to me like a seniors' dance venue than a place I'd go to shake my groove thing. I wouldn't have said that to Vera, though.

"It's enchanting, and we danced for hours."

"Has Paul said anything . . . ?" I waved my hand dismissively. "No, of course he hasn't. Never mind."

"Has he said anything about what?"

"About the Graham Stott investigation," I

said. "I just wonder what the local media consensus is on whether Blake and Todd are guilty."

"In general, pretty much everyone thinks they're guilty, including the media," Vera said. "Haven't you been keeping up with the daily write-ups?"

"No. I was afraid they'd only depress me," I said.

"You should reconsider. At least read Paul's articles. They're available online, and they're fair-minded. Paul has written some informative background articles this past week, as well as the articles detailing the crime, what police are saying, and all that."

"Thanks for letting me know, Vera. I'll look at them."

"Paul is very talented," she said. "And I'm not saying that only because we're dating."

At five, I locked up the shop and put the clock sign on the door indicating I'd be back at five thirty. I normally close the shop at five on Friday, but I wanted Andy to know that I'd be returning in case he arrived there before I made it back. Even though I wanted to stress to him that this was a friendship dinner and not a date, I didn't want him to think I'd stood him up.

I took Angus home, fed him, and let him out into the backyard. Then I jogged upstairs and changed my T-shirt for a nice blouse.

When I pulled up to the shop, I saw that Andy's yellow Camaro was already there. I quickly unlocked the door, removed the clock sign, and then relocked the door.

Andy pulled up beside the sidewalk. "Ready to go?"

"Yes," I said. "I'll follow you in my Jeep."

"Why can't you ride with me?"

"I have to get up early in the morning to come to work," I said. "I thought that by taking separate cars, we could cut down on the drive time by eliminating an extra trip here."

He shrugged. "Whatever you think. Is the Italian place in Depoe Bay all right with you?"

"That'll be fine." I smiled. "Lead the way."

I could tell he wasn't happy about the arrangement, but after he went kind of nuts on me yesterday, I wanted him to be absolutely certain that all we were having together this evening was dinner.

The Italian bistro—called Bistro Bella—in Depoe Bay wasn't anything fancy, but the food smelled delicious. As soon as that aroma wafted in my direction, I realized I hadn't eaten lunch today. Small square tables adorned with blue-and-white-checked tablecloths filled the dining room. Each table was designed to accommodate four diners, and a couple of larger parties had pushed two or three of the tables together.

Andy and I found an available table and sat down. A waitress came over and asked what she could bring us to drink. I ordered a diet soda, and Andy requested a beer. She left, and Andy and I looked at each other, struggling for something to say.

"Did you have a nice day at school today?" I asked, realizing a fraction too late that the question made me sound like his mother.

"Yeah . . . thanks," he said. "Did you have a good day?"

"It was okay." I looked around at some of the other diners. There was a couple who had two children—a little girl who appeared to be about six years old and a boy in a high chair who was only a few months old. I smiled at the baby. "He's so cute."

The waitress brought our drinks.

I thought of something else I could say. "I understand Tawny changed her name to Sarah. Did you call her Sarah or Tawny?"

"She was always Tawny to me," Andy said.

"What did Drew think of your calling his mother Tawny instead of Sarah?" I asked. "Didn't he think that was odd?"

He shook his head. "We told him it was a nickname. And, of course, that made sense to him because his Grampa John also called her Tawny."

"Right," I said. "That makes sense. I have to say, though, that I'm sorry I nosed into everyone's past. I had no right to do that, and now I feel like a complete heel."

"Aw, you're being too hard on yourself," he said. "You were concerned about your friends, and you were trying to help. Anyone could understand that. Besides, I'm sorta glad you got involved. If you hadn't, we wouldn't be friends now."

I smiled. "I'm glad about that part too."

"Let's not talk about depressing stuff tonight," said Andy. "You know something about my college days. Why don't you tell me about yours?"

Before I could think of something to tell him, the waitress returned to take our order. I was glad because it gave me time to think of something funny.

"Well, Sadie and I were roommates in college," I said. "Sadie's mom is as sweet as can be, but she was like a helicopter—she was always hovering. As a matter of fact, I think she might still be that way. Anyway, it was hard for her to deal with her baby girl being in college. And Sadie was having a pretty hard time trying to deal with being in college herself."

Andy smiled. "I knew her through Blake, but she didn't say much about her academic career."

"She changed majors more than once. In fact, she'd already been there a year when I was a freshman. I think her parents thought she was going to major in everything and be in college until they went bankrupt."

"How about you?" he asked. "Did you always know what you wanted to do?"

"Not in the least. But I knew I was good with numbers, so I went with accounting. I'd dreamed of opening my own business, but I never thought it would happen." I sipped my soda. "Anyway, one night after Sadie had been particularly stressed-out and depressed, I decided to throw her a pity party. I mean, she'd been in the dumps all week, and I thought enough was enough."

"And you actually threw her a party?"

"I did." I laughed. "I invited a bunch of girls

who lived in the dorm with us, and they all brought silly stuff like Kleenex, and diapers, and baby food, because they wanted to make it obvious they thought Sadie was acting like a baby."

"Was Sadie mad?" Andy asked.

"Not until her mother called," I said. "I didn't know it was Mrs. Van Huss. I was thinking it was one of the girls who hadn't got to the party yet. Did I mention there were wine coolers involved?"

"What did you do when Mrs. Van Huss called?" He was grinning, already anticipating my mortifying response.

I bit my lip. "I answered the phone, *Hi, Madame Sadie's House of Satisfaction. What's your pleasure?*"

Andy's jaw dropped and then he dissolved into a fit of laughter. "What did Mrs. Van Huss say?"

"What did she *say*? Nothing. I didn't even know it was her until she called Sadie back and demanded an explanation. She merely screeched and slammed down the phone on me," I said. "And *that* is what snapped Sadie out of her depression. That, and the fact that she and Blake made up the next day." I thought a minute. That's why she'd been depressed. She and Blake had had a horrible fight and

THE LONG STITCH GOOD NIGHT 303

broken up. They didn't speak to each other for over a week. I thought their relationship was over for good. That must've been when Blake had the one-nighter with Tawny.

Andy was still laughing over the incident, but I was racking my brain to remember what time of year that had been. It was cold . . . I remembered that much. And we'd delivered the diapers and baby food to a local women's shelter the next day. When we arrived, the administrator was taking down the New Year's decorations that had been up over the weekend. New Year's Day had been Saturday.

I was guessing that Blake's indiscretion with Tawny probably took place around the time of some sort of New Year's Eve drinking binge. If that was the case, and if Blake was the father of Tawny's child, then Drew should have been born in October.

"Is everything all right?" Andy asked. "You're looking solemn all of a sudden, and we decided we weren't going to be depressed this evening."

"I'm not," I said with a smile. "My mind just drifted to Drew. He's a beautiful child. When's his birthday?"

"December 30. He's a Capricorn. I'm an Aries—my birthday is March 25. When's yours?"

"My birthday is in August. I'm a Virgo," I said. "Did Tawny have any problems with the pregnancy? I've heard first births can be really tough."

"Not at all. She carried Drew to full term, and he was healthy and happy." He inclined his head. "Why all the questions about Drew?"

"I feel sorry for him. I mean, it's great that he's got you, and his grandfather, and Charles, but he's lost his mom. That's bound to be tough. It would be on anyone, but—"

"Charles?" Andy interrupted.

"Yeah . . . um . . . Tawny was married to Charles Siegel."

"Charles Siegel," he murmured. "All along, Tawny was married to Charlie?"

"Would you excuse me just a minute?" I asked. "I need to go to the ladies' room." I got up, retrieved my purse, and walked down the hall toward the bathroom. One, I was mortified that I'd dropped this bomb on Andy, but, two, I was desperate to let Blake know he was in the clear. For the umpteenth time, I tried to call Blake. And for the umpteenth time, my call went straight to voice mail.

"Blake," I said, my voice urgent. "Drew's birthday is December 30. No way." Then I hung up. Hopefully, that was cryptic enough to slide by Sadie if she happened to overhear the message.

I gathered up the nerve to return to the table. As had been the norm today, I'd said something stupid and caused someone to be hurt. I really needed to go home, crawl into bed, and stay there for the rest of the weekend. Or, at the very least, I needed to duct-tape my mouth shut.

Our food arrived, and I tried to make small talk while we ate. But Andy was distracted. As soon as dinner was over, he paid the waitress and we went our separate ways.

I wished I hadn't offhandedly mentioned Tawny's marriage to Charles. It didn't make sense that Tawny wouldn't have told Andy who she was married to. And why wouldn't she have told Charles she'd remained friends with Andy? Had she been afraid Charles would feel threatened by their friendship? Or maybe Andy and Charles had never gotten along all that well, and that's why she hadn't told them about each other. Either way, with Tawny dead, Drew could use as many caring and supportive people as he could get in his life.

Chapter Twenty-one

When I turned down the street to my house, I could see the MacKenzies' Mochas van in my driveway. Blake usually drove the van, and Sadie drove their BMW convertible. I pulled in beside the van. Blake was sitting in the driver's seat just staring into space. When I got out of the car, he got out of the van.

"Blake, are you all right?" I asked.

He shrugged.

"Please tell me you haven't been drinking," I said.

"I haven't." At my skeptical expression, he breathed in my face. His breath wasn't minty fresh, but it didn't smell like alcohol. "See?"

"Thanks for that," I said, raising an eyebrow.

"Made you believe me, didn't it?" He grinned.

"You could've given me a *cross my heart* or a *Scout's honor* or something." I unlocked the door and flipped on the light. "Does Sadie know you're here?"

"She doesn't know where I am. When I left your shop, I called her and told her I needed to clear my head. I told her that with her parents at our house and people thronging the coffeehouse to gawk at the killer, the stress was too much for me and that I needed to get away for a little while."

"'A little while'?" I asked. "That was hours ago. She's bound to be worried sick."

"How did you figure out I'm not the father of Tawny Milligan's son?" he asked.

"I remembered when you and Sadie had that falling-out and broke up for about a week. It was around New Year's. I figured that's when you and Tawny . . . you know . . . reconnected." I put my purse and keys on the hall table and avoided Blake's eyes. "Andy said Drew's birthday was December 30. That's how I knew it didn't add up."

"Andy?" Blake scrunched up his nose. "What were you doing with Andy?"

"He asked me to have dinner with him. And I went—as friends. I felt like I owed him that, since I was so deceitful with him when I asked him to dinner to see what he knew about Graham's murder." I told Blake to go ahead and have a seat while I let Angus in.

I went through the kitchen to the back door and opened it for Angus. He bounded inside and jumped up to give me a hug. Afterward, he followed me into the living room. When he saw Blake sitting on the sofa, he ran over, placed his front paws on Blake's knees, and began licking his face.

"Thanks. I love you too," Blake said, trying to avoid Angus's slurps.

I went back to the kitchen and got Angus a chew toy. "Here, baby."

He scrambled off Blake's lap to get his treat.

"You were right about the timing," Blake said. "That *is* when I got together with Tawny. We were at a party, we'd both been drinking, I thought it was all over with Sadie. . . ." He sighed. "It was a huge mistake. Drew *could* have been mine. I was stupid."

"Everybody does stupid things. It's over now."

"Not entirely. I have to tell Sadie," he said.

"I'm not sure that's wise," I said. Yes, I was

surprised at myself for saying that because I felt strongly that couples should be completely honest with each other, but . . . "That's way in the past. It's irrelevant now. Wouldn't it be better to let it go than to hurt Sadie with it now?"

"Maybe, but if she finds out from someone else, she'll be even more hurt. And she'll resent me for not telling her." He looked up at the ceiling. "You know we've had our trust issues in the past. I don't want her doubting me. I have to tell her."

"Well, you can't tell her with her parents there," I said. "This is definitely not something they need to know."

"It can't wait."

"Then call her and have her come here." I handed Blake my phone. "When she gets here, I'll leave you two alone."

Blake took the phone, and I went into the kitchen to make a pot of decaf coffee. I figured they could use it.

When Sadie arrived, she was a little bewildered. She wasn't sure what she was doing there. I told her that Blake thought the two of them could use some time to talk privately and that he and I didn't know where they might be able to accomplish that other than here. Then I gave Sadie a hug, and Angus and I went upstairs to my bedroom.

I slipped off my shoes and stifled a yawn as I propped myself up in bed with the television remote. Angus climbed up and lay down beside me. I clicked on the TV and surfed around the channels trying to find something interesting. Of course, my mind was in large part with Sadie and Blake downstairs. I was relieved when the phone rang because, no matter who was calling, I'd have to concentrate on the call.

Fortunately, it wasn't a telemarketer. It was Todd.

"Hey," he said softly. "I'm sorry for getting angry and leaving the shop in a huff today."

"I'm sorry I was bossy and interfering," I said. "The investigation is really none of my business, and I wound up causing more problems than I solved."

"No. You were right, Marcy. I do need to take some responsibility and get more involved in the murder investigation. In fact, I talked with my attorney, and we're going to set up a meeting with the police."

"I'm glad. I hope you can help them find the person who killed Graham."

"I suppose I was just hoping the whole situation would resolve itself," Todd said. "I mean,

Blake and I are innocent, and I thought that would be proven in the end. But the circumstantial evidence kept mounting up. After I left the Seven-Year Stitch, I realized I did need to be more proactive in defending myself."

"Well, then, I'm happy my bad mood rubbed off on you in a good way," I told him.

"When we're finished talking, I'm going to call Blake and suggest he do the same thing."

"Um . . . you might want to hold off on that for tonight," I said. "Blake and Sadie are downstairs."

"Downstairs? They're at your place? What happened?"

I gave Todd a brief rundown of the situation.

"I hope they're able to work everything out and put this behind them," Todd said.

"So do I. I feel like it's another fine mess I've gotten everyone into."

"Come on, Marce. Don't you think you're being a little hard on yourself?" he asked. "You didn't cause any of this. You might've revealed it, but you didn't cause it."

"Yeah, I guess you're right. Still, if they're not hunky-dory fine, it's not going to make me feel any less crummy."

Not long after I talked with Todd, I heard Sadie's car leave. A few minutes later, I heard the van start up. I went downstairs to make sure the coffeepot had been turned off. It had been, even though the coffee hadn't been touched.

I said a silent prayer for my friends before going back upstairs.

Despite getting little sleep, I woke up early Saturday morning. I took Angus for a jog on the beach. Then we came home, I took a bath, and we still got to the shop an hour before we were scheduled to open. I put my tote and purse in my office. I saw the dumbbells and considered working my arms, but I decided maybe later. I wasn't feeling *that* energetic.

I took my embroidery project to the sit-and-stitch square, and Angus found one of his chew toys. It was immediately forgotten, though, when he looked out the window and saw a familiar face he hadn't seen in a while. Manu.

Angus jumped against the glass and began barking.

Manu and Reggie were walking past with a to-go bag from MacKenzies' Mochas. They were an adorable couple, despite the fact that they were so different. While Reggie dressed in somewhat traditional Indian apparel, Manu preferred Western dress—he was practically a cowboy with his jeans, flannel shirts, and boots.

They came into the shop, and Reggie had to hold the bag up near her ear to keep it from being knocked out of her hand by the bouncing, excited dog. I took the bag from her and put it on the counter.

"He's missed you," I said to Manu. "And so have I."

"I've missed all of you," he said, giving his wife a one-armed hug.

Reggie nodded toward the bag. "That's for you. Blake sent it."

"Okay." I wanted to see what it was, but I didn't want to be rude. "Come and sit down. Tell me about your trip, Manu."

"Well, I'm sure Reggie has already told you the good parts," Manu said. "Then tragedy struck, and I had to stay behind and help settle my uncle's affairs. My father has been dead for several years now, and so I'm the man of the family where my mother is concerned."

"It's good you could be there to help her," I said.

"It was," he agreed. "But now I'm glad to be back at home . . . even if I *can't* turn my back on you people for an instant."

I smiled. "Hey, it wasn't me this time."

"No, but I hear you're up to your neck in it just the same." His heavy-lidded eyes regarded me shrewdly.

"I can't help myself," I admitted. "I want to fix things."

"Fix embroidery things. Leave investigating crimes to the police," he said.

Behind his back, Reggie rolled her eyes. She knew I wasn't capable of that. Maybe I'd missed my calling. Maybe I could be Marcy Singer, embroidering private eye. Another noir fantasy started forming in my brain, but I quickly put it out of my head.

"Speaking of the investigation, you haven't been briefed on it yet, have you?" I asked.

"No." Manu grinned. "I was going to go to the station later this morning. But if you'd like to go ahead and brief me now, Detective Singer, feel free."

I blushed. "That's all right. I think I'll leave it to the professionals."

Manu looked at Reggie. "Put that on the calendar, my love. Marcy said she'd leave something to the professionals. That's bound to be a first."

"And likely a last," Reggie said with a wink in my direction.

We chatted awhile longer, and then Reggie

and Manu had to leave. He was supposed to be at the station by eleven a.m. After they'd left, I opened the small bag that was still on the counter. Inside were a cinnamon raisin muffin and a note from Blake, which read *Thanks for letting us borrow your living room.*

I didn't know if that meant everything had turned out okay or not. I decided to pretend it had . . . at least, unless and until I learned that it hadn't.

Approximately an hour after Reggie and Manu left, a bus full of seniors rolled into the square. The bus doors whooshed open, and older folks with sunglasses, fanny packs, and orthopedic sneakers fanned out in all directions. After the bus's occupants had all disembarked, the driver closed the doors and pulled around the back of the shops so the bus wouldn't be in anyone's way.

I was happy I—and the other merchants would have plenty of business today. But, boy, was I glad Blake had sent me a muffin. I was going to need all the energy I could get.

Three hours later, I stood in the doorway waving at the departing busload of seniors. They were smiling, talking to each other, and waving to me and the other shop owners as they boarded, bags in hand. They'd been a lot of fun and had been wonderfully generous in their spending. Plus, they'd had many fascinating stories to regale everyone with. I truly enjoyed having them in the Seven-Year Stitch today.

When I turned back and looked at my shop, though, it was a mess. I went to my office and got a steno pad so I could make notes about what I needed to restock from the storeroom. That would also help me keep track of what I was running low on in the storeroom so I could reorder.

I needed to restock all my kits, many colors of embroidery floss, yarn, fabric, monk's cloth, needles, and frames. I took two of my canvas shopping baskets into the storeroom, got as much as I could carry in one trip, and checked those items off. As I restocked, I put the shelves back in order. Three trips later, I was done. I saw that I needed to reorder fabric, frames, hoops, and tapestry needles. I was low on kits, but I was expecting some new ones to come in sometime in the coming week.

After I'd finished, I flopped onto the sofa with a soda and a bag of baked barbecue chips. Angus was snoozing in the corner. He was so tired that he didn't even raise his head at the sound of the chip bag being opened.

My phone buzzed, indicating I had a text. It was from Blake.

I need to see you. It's URGENT. Meet me at the lighthouse, and please don't tell Sadie where you're going. Thanks, Blake.

Chapter Twenty-two

I closed up the shop, and Angus and I went out to get into the Jeep. It was only four thirty, but Blake had said he needed to see me urgently. Why he didn't want to meet at my house was beyond me. It would have been a lot better than a practically deserted lighthouse on a cloudy, windy March afternoon.

I wasn't watching where I was going when I stepped out the door, and I nearly ran into Todd.

He put out his hands to steady me. "Where's the fire?"

"It's at the lighthouse," I said. "I mean, there isn't a fire, but I have to meet Blake. I don't know what's going on, but Blake said it was urgent and not to tell Sadie where I was going.

Things must not have worked out well last night after all."

"Do you want me to come with you?" he asked.

"No. He probably feels that I've betrayed him enough as it is without knowing I confided his problems to you." I raised and dropped a shoulder. "No offense."

"None taken. Just call and let me know if there's anything I can do . . . for either of you," he said.

"Thanks I will." I put Angus into the Jeep, not bothering with the restraint. I drove as quickly as the curvy, narrow road to the lighthouse would allow. When I got there, I saw the MacKenzies' Mochas van in the parking lot. Blake wasn't inside.

Angus was still pooped from the tourists' visit, and he was lying in the backseat panting. I rolled all the windows down and left him in the Jeep. Since the Jeep and Blake's van were the only vehicles in sight, and since I was planning to come back for Angus as soon as I'd located Blake, I thought he'd be okay.

I started up the gravel path to the black and white lighthouse. "Blake! It's Marcy! Where are you?"

I listened as I continued to walk, but there

was no answer. When I got closer, I tried again. "Blake!"

"Marcy! What's wrong?" He came around the side of the lighthouse.

"Nothing's wrong with me. What's wrong with you?" I asked.

"I got your message. You said it was urgent that I meet you here."

I frowned and shook my head. "No, I got *your* message."

Charles Siegel came around the other side of the lighthouse. "Actually, you both got *my* message. I didn't know whether you'd come to assist me, but I knew you'd come to each other's aid."

"You could've just asked," I said. "And why did you want to meet here?"

"Because it's the off-season, and I didn't want us to be interrupted," Charles said. "What I'm about to say cannot be repeated." He looked from me to Blake and back again.

Blake and I both murmured our consent.

"I have to tell you I was relieved when Graham Stott was murdered. He'd long been a thorn in my side," said Charles. "I'd wanted to adopt Drew ever since I married his mother seven years ago. I looked into it and saw that she and I would have to petition the court for adoption and that we'd have to have the birth father's permission. Sarah wouldn't let me ask Graham for permission."

"Because he wasn't really the birth father," I said.

Charles flattened his lips. "I know that now. Why she didn't tell me that then is beyond me. I didn't have any idea until last Friday night when I called John Milligan to tell him the news about Graham. I told him I no longer had an obstacle to the adoption because Graham had been shot and killed. That's when I heard for the first time that it wasn't possible for Graham to be the father and that the attorney had forbidden Sarah from using the Stott surname."

"You'd been married seven years, and she never told you that?" I asked.

"No. . . . Her past was a particularly sticky subject between us. She'd changed her name and buried her past, and I preferred that it never be resurrected." Charles sighed. "Maybe if I'd been more forgiving of her past, she'd have trusted me with the truth. I don't know."

I wondered if Sadie had been forgiving of Blake's past and thought that, if not, she could learn something from Charles's sad tale. And then another thought struck me: Charles called John Milligan on Friday night?

"Anyway, after John told me about Graham, I tried my best to remember who'd been with Tawny—or, rather, Sarah—around the time she got pregnant," Charles continued. "We'd buried her past so deeply that I had no idea. I have to confess, Blake, I'm the one who broke into your house the night of the shooting and stole your OSU yearbook and some of your other alumni papers. I wanted to see if my wife might've written something in the *Beaver* hinting at who she'd been involved with. Or I thought that if you were the guy she'd been with, maybe you'd kept articles that had been about her for sentimental reasons or something." He raised and dropped his hands. "Other than answers about Drew's possible paternity, I had no idea what I was looking for."

"Charlie, you could've just asked me for the book," Blake said. "For that matter, you could've just asked me if I was the father of Tawny's child."

"It's irrelevant now," said Charles. "I know you are."

"No I'm not," Blake told him emphatically.

"But you and Sadie had the argument." Charles's eyes darted from Blake to me. "Marcy remembered that. You'd broken up for a week or so. Didn't you get back together with Tawny—I mean, Sarah—at that time?"

"Yes. I mean, no. We didn't get back to-gether." Blake looked down at the sand, find-ing it difficult to talk to Charles about a tryst he'd once had with the man's now-deceased wife. "It was a onetime thing. We were drunk, and we regretted it immediately."

"Still, that one night was enough to produce Drew," Charles said. "All I'm asking is that you sign over your parental rights. Then I can raise Drew as my own son . . . as I have for the past seven years. With Sarah dead and with-out me being granted legal guardianship over Drew, he and I have a tenuous arrangement. I wouldn't even be able to sign him into a hospi-tal if he got sick."

"I'm telling you, Charlie, I am not Drew's father," Blake insisted. "Tawny and I slept to-gether the first week in January. Marcy said Drew was born at the end of December."

Charles drew a shuddering breath. "Please. Just sign your rights away. Then John will tes-tify that I've been a good father to the boy, and the judge will grant me custody."

"Do the math!" Blake yelled. "I'm not the boy's biological father!"

"You are!" Charles shouted. "I don't care about the math! All I care about is gaining cus-tody of my child!" He held his arms toward

Blake. "Please, man. Just sign a paper. It'll be all right."

"It won't," Blake said softly. "I'd do anything I could to help you, Charlie, but the court might require a paternity test. And I'm *not* Drew's biological father."

"Can't you petition the court and say the identity of the father is unknown and that you've raised the child with his mother for the past seven years?" I asked quickly. Like Blake, I really wanted to help this poor guy get custody of his son. "You know Riley Kendall. She's a wonderful attorney. I'm sure she'd take your case."

Charles stepped toward me. He got so close that when he screamed at me, his spit flew in my face. It was disgusting. "You think everything can be solved if you poke around in it, don't you? You think you're such a genius! Well, you're not! You're a freakin' screwup! Why didn't you just let this all go? Why did you have to make it worse?" He grabbed me by the shoulders.

Blake stepped between us. "That's enough. None of this is Marcy's fault. This is between you and me."

I looked beyond Blake and Charles and saw that Angus had climbed out the window of the Jeep and was running toward us furiously. I started to head him off, but Charles jerked me backward. I tripped and fell in the sand. As I struggled to my feet, Charles noticed the dog. He took a pistol from his jacket pocket and aimed it at Angus.

"No!" I screamed. I dived at Charles as he fired. I knocked his arm upward, so his shot went high.

Blake grabbed Charles's wrist and slammed it against the lighthouse wall until Charles loosened his grip on the gun so Blake could take it away from him.

Sobbing, I ran to Angus. He was standing just a short distance away from us, and he was—as far as I could tell—fine. I buried my face in his neck and held him as tightly as I could.

I heard feet pounding on the path, and I looked up to see Ted and Todd racing toward us. Since Blake still had Charles pinned against the lighthouse, Ted went to confiscate the gun and handcuff Charles.

"Careful with that gun," Blake said. "I think you'll find that it's the one that killed Graham Stott."

"Marcy, are you all right?" Todd asked, bending down to see about me.

Angus growled.

"Back away," I said. "Please. He's scared . . . and he might be hurt."

Todd did as I asked, and put some distance between us. "I don't see any blood on the ground."

"I don't either." I ran my hands gingerly over Angus's torso. I didn't see any blood, and he didn't flinch at my touch. "I believe he's all right. Just scared."

"And you're trembling like the last leaf of autumn," Ted said, leading Charles in a wide arc away from Angus and me. "Will you be okay to drive yourself home?"

I nodded.

"Then take Angus on to the house," he said. "Blake, you and Todd follow me to the station. Marcy, I'll come by to get your statement later."

"Thanks." I stood, took Angus by the collar, and led him to the Jeep. Hopefully we could all begin closing the book on this fiasco.

It was about nine p.m. by the time Ted got to the house to take my statement. He told me Todd had come to the station a few minutes after running into me on the sidewalk. He'd felt something was off about the way Blake had sent me an urgent message asking me to meet him and telling me not to mention it to Sadie. Todd went on to MacKenzies' Mochas and asked Sadie where Blake was. She said he got an urgent message and went to help a friend. That's all she knew. Now convinced something weird was going on, Todd went by the police station to get Ted before coming to the lighthouse.

"Charles Siegel had already come on our radar as a suspect in the murder," Ted told me. "More than one person said he shoved them out of the way in order to get away from the back room immediately following the shooting. They simply thought he was scared, but we thought it was worth looking into."

"What makes me the sickest is that none of this needed to have happened for Charles to get what he wanted," I said. "It's like I told him—he could've said he wanted custody of the child and that the paternity was unknown. The authorities would have looked at the birth certificate, seen Graham Stott listed as the father, and contacted Graham about his parental rights. But Graham wouldn't have opposed Charles. And now Drew is without a father."

"I guess Charles was afraid Graham would claim the boy, since he didn't know Graham wasn't the biological father," said Ted. "But you're wrong about Drew not having a father."

Epilogue

It was a sunny day in early April when a little boy I recognized from his photo as Drew Masterson came running into my shop. He was as delighted to meet Angus as Angus was to meet him. The child was smiling and happy. No one would have guessed that his mom had died and that the man he'd known as his father would be going on trial for murder soon. Andy and I had remained friends, mainly because Andy credited me for helping to bring him and Drew together as father and son.

"Hey, Uncle Andy, look!" he called.

"I told you that you'd love Angus," Andy said.

"Andy, come on into my office and pick out sodas for you and Drew," I said.

"I'll be right back, buddy. Behave yourself." Andy followed me into my office.

"Did you get the test results back yet?" I asked.

He nodded. "He's all mine." He beamed. "I think on some level I knew all along. Sure, Tawny and I remained close friends, but I think my being Drew's real father was part of that. She wanted the two of us to be close. I should've asked her about it, but I was afraid to. I didn't want to upset the applecart."

"Will you tell Drew you're his dad?" I asked.

"When he's ready. He and I have moved in with his grandpa John for the time being," he said. "John has a fenced backyard, and my landlord didn't allow dogs."

I told him to help himself to the minifridge, and he took out two mango juices. We went back into the office and watched Drew romping happily with the dog. On the wall behind where Drew and Angus were playing hung the Mount mellick piece that I'd finished just the day before.

I smiled as I remembered another Marilyn Monroe quote: *I believe that everything happens for a reason. People change so that you can learn to let go, things go wrong so that you appreciate them when they're right, you believe lies so you eventually learn to trust no one but yourself, and sometimes good things fall apart so better things can fall together.*

ABOUT THE AUTHOR

Amanda Lee lives in southwest Virginia with her husband and two beautiful children, a boy and a girl. She's a full-time writer/editor/mom/wife and chief cook and bottle washer, and she loves every minute of it. Okay, not the bottle washing so much, but the rest of it is great.

CONNECT ONLINE
www.gayletrent.com